BONES ON THE MOUNTAIN

A Mountain Protectors Novel

Mindy Steele

A

ALLY PRESS

Print ISBN: 978-1-953290-15-1
eBook ISBN: 978-1-953290-16-8

Printed in the United States

The characters in *Bones on the Mountain* will capture your heart from the first page. Then Mindy Steele did what good suspense authors do—she put them in a run for their lives that will have the reader turning pages to find out what happens next.

I can't wait for the next book!

Patricia Bradley,
Winner of Inspirational
Reader's Choice Award

Mindy Steele crafts a story filled with interesting characters, page-turning suspense and a bit of romance. You will enjoy this one!

Mary Ellis,
USA Today bestselling author

As a Kentucky girl, I am always on the lookout for books set in the Bluegrass. I was excited to find Mindy Steeler's latest. Bones on the Mountain does not disappoint! Not only does the story beautifully capture the connection between the land and the people who love it, but it does so in a way that keeps readers turning pages. Fans of southern fiction, suspense, and romance will adore this story!"

Beth Pugh,
author of the *Pine Valley Holiday* Series

CHAPTER ONE

The Fall
Life is a series of falls and each one, necessary.

Samantha Quinn stretched out the stiffness as the twelve-hour shift waned to an end. Ten years working as a first responder 911dispatcher for the Milford County Sheriff's office did nothing to make sitting long hours any easier. It wasn't physical work like running the seasonal hunting lodge, but it did require a lot more focus, a disconnect from common human reactions, and too many hours sitting in a chair.

Behind the large grey desk, the heart of the nerve center, she glanced at each of the three monitors finally resting. It had been a long shift, even here in Milford. Hopefully Monty, the day shift dispatcher, would get here on time. She had her doubts considering Monty never hurried at a thing.

The old radiator popped in the far corner, echoing eerily around the concrete basement room. There was a small bathroom and a single cell situated down a narrow hall. It was rarely used now that offenders were carted off to the next county and the jailer retired.

Upstairs, Ron and his deputies worked. The sheriff's office had full lighting and windows and it didn't smell at all like a forgotten old cellar. Maybe next year's budget would give them an upgrade to that floor, she hoped.

Noting it was nearing seven, Sam adjusted her left ear corded headset. Some dispatchers preferred the double ear muffs snugged to their ears or the right ear version. Sam preferred her signature tool of choice to hear more than what the deputies randomly squawked about.

The ringing of the phone pulled her back to first responder mode.

"911, where's your emergency?" Asking where, instead of what, gave the dispatcher a jump on sending help quickly. If the caller was unable to do more than answer one of the required questions, location was key.

"The deer ran straight into me. Came from out of nowhere and hit me," the voice was female, young, and mildly frantic. *A vehicle accident,* Sam mentally noted and began typing onto the keyboard, logging the information into the CAD system, Computer Aided Dispatch.

"This door won't budge." The girl grunted and Sam knew she was trying to get out of the vehicle. Adrenaline was an enemy to common sense in an emergency and few had learned to master it.

"Calm down ma'am. I need your location to send help. Do you know where you are?"

"Uh, I'm somewhere between work and home. This door won't open." Sam took a slow breath. Emotions didn't occupy this atmosphere. Every scenario was fuel used to sharpen skills. That's how lives were saved. A dispatcher who didn't try, who sat in this chair for a paycheck, cost lives. That's why she was here, away from her son and her beloved mountain, because from the day she had turned thirteen, Samantha Quinn knew firsthand what a sleepy unskilled dispatcher could do in a life or death situation.

"I'm in a yard. I'm… Oh God, I tore down the Sutton's fence. He's going to kill me," the girl began cursing obscenities. That too came with the job.

"Are you hurt?" Sam asked next determining her state of injuries.

"Not unless pride counts?" Sam quirked a grin at the humor.

"My screen is showing you are on Parker Road. Does that sound right?"

"Yes."

"I know where you are sweetie. I'm sending help, but don't hang up." Sam quickly radioed David who would be coming onto his morning shift any minute. The newly hired deputy, Alex Cane, had a long enough night breaking up two scratching females at the Brick, and a domestic that lasted longer than it should have for two people who felt the need to break all their personal possessions in the heat of rage. Mrs. Florence liked the heat on and Mr. Florence thought it was a waste of money in November.

"Unit thirty-one, we have a 10-45, location is 2370 Parker Road near the Eric Sutton residence. Female is coherent but unable to exit the vehicle." A non-injury vehicle accident but despite the driver saying she wasn't injured didn't mean that to be true. Next Sam called EMS, then one quick call to Matt, the local fire chief. Protocol was to always be followed.

"What is your name?" Sam continued logging into CAD keeping the girl on the line.

"Jenna. Jenna Spencer." Some victims yelled, enhancing a response and Sam adjusted her headset volume.

"Jenna, Deputy Schiffer and emergency responders are on the way. Stay in the car and..."

"Well I can't get out, so that's not going to be a problem." Jenna sighed heavily. "You're not going to call my mom are you? I am nineteen now Sam Quinn," her voice clipped. Small town life revealed few strangers.

"Just wonderful," Jenna growled into her cell phone. "Mr. Sutton is coming out of his house and he doesn't look happy. Can you go to hell for crashing into a preacher's yard and damaging his property?" Sam resisted an amused grin.

"No Jenna, only if you did it on purpose," Sam responded lightly.

"Good to know. I hear the sirens, can I hang up now?" Tough gal, Sam thought, and smiled. She would make a great dispatcher someday.

"Yes dear. And might I suggest you call your mom. Sybil will find out. Don't make your momma worry when she gets word her daughter was in an accident."

"I know and if they cut me loose from this blasted car, I will, but not until I know my legs can outrun hers. They're still shaking and she is going to kill me if the preacher doesn't first. It's her car!" The phone went dead and Sam let the laugh fill the small concrete room.

Footsteps sounded down the steep stairwell outside, light and quick, and certainly not the heavy thuds of Monty's two-hundred plus frame. Sam glanced at the camera screen, installed just two years previous now that the dispatch center had NCIC, National Crime Information Center, access from the Federal Bureau of Investigations. Only those in law enforcement could now enter this room. Noting Connie, her friend and supervisor, descending the stairs, Sam shoved her hunting magazine collection aside, and gave them a quick tuck under the dummy sheet for less seasoned dispatchers. Connie would spat on again how women didn't read North American Whitetail and Hunting magazine over Country Sampler or Woman's Day. "It's not normal," Connie contended. Sam didn't do normal, and wasn't it important to keep up with trends and hunting tips, stay in line with bigger ranches and hunting preserves when you owned one? Besides, Sam found those last page personal stories that hunters wrote about bagging a big one or mishaps on the hunt, preferred reading.

Connie opened the timeworn door supporting two cups of fresh coffee in a paper tray. A waft of cold November air rushed into the room like a gift.

"Happy vacation," Connie sang with a huge smile and handed her one of the cups. "Might I suggest this year besides escorting men with guns up and down mountains you add something more accept-able for a single woman to your vacation agenda."

Sam wasn't doing whatever Connie deemed acceptable. Vacations were for work. Sam had clients and a website to keep updated with pictures of nice bucks. Vacations were also time for helping Nelly in the kitchen. Though Sam's mother-in-law had a thing about too many women in one kitchen, when the lodge was full with hungry hunters, Nelly often grew tired enough to let Sam try out new recipes.

"Thank you. I needed this, and no, it's work for me as usual." Sam sipped, letting the warm energy burst slip down her throat. Yes, a vacation was sorely needed. Three weeks of hauling hunters around Bear Claw Mountain and entertaining them with pictures and fine food was just what she needed. From the first cold morn-ing of open firearm season until the last meal, it was fresh air and mingling with those who paid handsomely for their food and lodg-ing. Most even left with a recipe tucked in their suitcases in hopes their spouses would find it appealing. Nelly had mastered taking a deer roast and preparing it into a gourmet dish of pungent herbs and moist meat and it had quickly become a last-night-at-the-lodge meal favorite.

The Deer Creek Lodge had been Dale's dream, not hers, but after her husband's death, she couldn't simply walk away. Guilt wouldn't allow for that. Nor could she leave Nelly with a two-story empty house and eight-hundred and seventy acre farm. The Quinn Matriarch had buried a husband and all three of her children. Sam couldn't leave her and if she was being honest, in five years she'd developed a happy routine. Something about the mountain, the changing of the seasons painting it in different colors, called to her like few things in life had. Being a dispatcher was a life of servitude. Her mountain, that was sanctuary.

"Any excitement last night?" Connie rounded the desk and leaned into it. If Sam wasn't mistaken, Connie was wearing makeup. Must be date night again, Sam recollected. Connie and Matt still did that, date night. It was cute and she couldn't blame any woman for keeping the marriage sparking. Not everyone was her, the woman who failed at being a wife.

"Not much. Deputy Cane had to break up Laini Berryman and Heather Brock down at the Brick around eleven. Something about Laini wearing a short skirt on purpose, just to get Heather's husband to notice." Sam's brow lifted over the coffee cup cradled at her mouth.

"Heather is a jealous woman and Laini does need to let out those hems. She's not thirty anymore," Connie huffed worming her way out of her red jersey jacket.

"The Florence's tore up their house over the thermostat setting." Connie lifted a brow. "Cane said when he got there the floors was littered with glass and broken furniture."

"Oh my." Connie responded but didn't sound surprised.

"When Cane went to leave, they were making out in front of him." Sam grinned. "He said he lived here all his life and could have gone without knowing that on Sunday he shared a pew with two crazy people." Sam laughed.

"Boy's got a lot of learning to do about married folk and what keeps things interesting," Connie wiggled her brows. "Let's not tell him about Mr. Richmond's hobbies. Might be interesting to see how the new deputy reacts to that one." Connie lifted her perfectly plucked brows taking her lightly tinted lips with it.

"I heard his neighbor Stella caught him howling from the ridge again yesterday." Sam informed.

"Sheryl didn't mention it when she left her shift." Connie sounded put off to have missed that tidbit of gossip.

"Nelly told me. At this point Stella doesn't even call it in anymore. Stella told her that if a man wants to strip down to nothing and howl at the moon, it's his privilege. I never would have taken him for a mental sort," Sam said twisting a lock of hair around her finger. "The man taught American history for Pete's sake."

"His wife is gone, kids grown, retired, and he's pushing seventy-nine. He could have always been mental for all we know, just now figured he can let loose of some of it. Besides, I have it on good authority, Stella bought some mighty expensive binoculars a few weeks back at the local sporting goods store," Connie said.

"You're kidding," Sam snickered trying to imagine Nelly's dear sixty-year-old friend playing peeping Tom out her kitchen window. "Oh, and Jenna Spencer just crashed Sybil's car into Eric Sutton's fence."

"Wow, you have been busy. Is she alright?" Connie glanced at the monitors.

"I think she's more upset about what Sybil will say than anything. I'm waiting for David to call back and confirm. It just happened."

"Sybil will be upset but praising God Jenna is okay. Fences can be mended, people can't, unless you're Lawson Montgomery. Dumb boy ruined another good vehicle Wednesday night and all he cared about was his foot. Terri will probably break his other one before the week's out."

"His foot?" Puzzled, Sam leaned on the far wall, crossed both boot covered ankles and waited for the newest scuttle in the rumor mill. A perk that came with the job was knowing the dish on the whole town.

"He got mad when he and his buddies couldn't pull his daddy's car out of the field past Watson's and kicked the tire, hard. He broke three toes for that temper of his. Monty sent Cane out there and he found Terri's car along with Seth Prichard's old Ford, a tractor that is believed to belong to old man Daulton up the road, that hasn't been confirmed yet, and Terri Montgomery dressed in a blue velvet robe and fuzzy slippers, tongue lashing all three teenagers. They called in Jake with the wrecker to pull all of them out, and you know Jake." Sam did know Jake.

"He thought it was the funniest thing ever." Sam mentally pictured the whole scene and had to admit, Terri in fuzzy slippers kicking up a fuss was pretty funny.

"That boy is the reason Terri's grey at forty-eight I tell you. If my boys did a fourth of the crazy stunts that one did I would give them to my mother-in-law to deal with."

"He might grow out of it. Boys can be stupid," Sam added, but hoped Brody was the exception.

"When Lawson was nine he ran away from home to join the X-men," Connie rolled her eyes. "Ron found him two hours later in the woods behind their house, soaked and crying scared. At eleven he tried stealing the neighbor's horse, got into a stretch of Bonanza staying after school with his grandmother." Sam remembered the horse incident and the look on Lawson's face when his mother had drug him into church every Sunday for two months after it.

"At fourteen, Quinn had to rescue him from that coyote. Dumb kid trapped it and couldn't figure out what to do with the darn thing afterward. Terri should have named him Trouble instead of Lawson." The phone rang and Connie picked up the headset and quickly donned it in place. "Drink the rest of your coffee and stretch, I'll take this one." Connie slid into the dispatcher chair with the fluency of water.

"911, where's your emergency?" Connie instantly plastered on her annoyed face. "Felicity I told you to stop calling every time someone threatens you for giving them a bad haircut. Have you ever considered another profession honey?" Connie was blunt to the tip. "No I don't think you need to be escorted to work because yesterday you ruined another head of hair," Connie blew out a hard breath.

Felicity Brown was the local hair stylist, a job she was not suited for by any means, and the town's former beauty queen. She won that title five years running with her red hair, sultry green eyes, and tight dresses with matching five-inch heels. Sam disliked her more than persimmons. It wasn't Christian, but there was no getting around it. Their dislike for each other was equally shared. It could have died out after high school but Felicity had a problem.

She didn't believe in vows or rings and it didn't disrupt her sleep taunting Sam that she was always the prettier choice if their paths crossed. Dale never could quite get over the redhead long after marrying Sam. Hindsight was a cruelty pressed upon the soul, because in the end, beauty had a power that no ring or vow did.

"Fine, I will send one of my deputies on over. You keep your paws off my officers now Felicity or I will add sexual harassment to it." Connie ended the call with a heavy sigh. "That woman will have those two-inch ruby red nails in poor Cane. He's too young. I'll send Schiffer." Sam giggled and sat her cup down on the desk as Connie called it in.

"Poor David, he looks like a lost man, unprepared for life as a single dad, a bachelor. I heard Crystal snagged a foot doctor over in Mason."

"If I see her again, she'll need him to help with removing one. What kind of woman leaves a man like David?" Connie spat. Sam kept her thoughts to herself.

Connie spun her chair and adjusted her earpiece. "You should go on, get some rest." Connie glanced at her watch. "Your vacation has now begun."

"Monty hasn't made it in, I'll wait. You're a supervisor, remember," Sam quirked.

"I know what I am and part of my job is to fill in if needed. We have a newbie too. Kate Carmichael just finished her paperwork and passed her background check. I think I will try her out while you're gone, see if she worth sending to EKU for her tele-communicators training. And you look beat. You're doing too much. Probably spent yesterday morning hiking that hill checking cameras again before you came on shift last night, didn't you?"

"It's my job," Sam repeated. "But no, I helped Nelly ready rooms, worked in my office first. We have nine coming the first week, six hunters and three wives. And that's after the three men from Georgia opening weekend," Sam expressed, "I even have the second week booked solid. It's our fullest year ever. Clark helps too."

Clark Quinn was Nelly's youngest nephew and since Dale's death had become a great help at the lodge. He maintained equipment, knew the trails, and helped chauffeur clients to their deer stands throughout opening weekend. He wasn't as skilled with a camera for those wanting their moment recorded, but he was muscle when it was needed and had CPR training, which was always a plus. Some men underestimated their abilities to climb a tree stand ladder.

"I'm glad he's there. I know Quinn stops by regular too."

Sam zipped up her jacket, but didn't respond to hearing Henry's name.

"You need to come out with us tonight. Celebrate your vacation. I bet I can even snag you a date from one of those new fellas down at the fire station," Connie teased.

"Not looking to snag." She pulled out her keys. Best to shut down this conversation before it started again. Just because her husband was dead didn't mean she wanted another. Life was good, safe, and predictable. Who needed romantic thoughts, broken promises, and future let-downs. She had a son, a career, a business, and the last thing Samantha Quinn needed in her life was a man to ruin it.

"Six years Samantha. It's time to forgive him." Connie narrowed a motherly scowl at her. Sam had forgiven Dale, it was her own stupidity she was having trouble with.

"I have," Sam admitted. "But..."

"You forget, I knew Dale before he plucked you up." Plucked her up was the way of it she guessed. Dale could have had any woman he wanted. Sam felt lucky he chose her until she learned luck was stupid and ran out faster than it came. If she hadn't been so lonely. So eager to fill a void. She let the always damaging thought go.

Connie stood and put both hands on Sam's shoulders. "It's a small town darling. We all know he wasn't much good as a husband." Sam felt a tear threaten but willed it to stay put.

"He had his way," she shrugged.

"To put it mildly," Connie agreed.

"I could have tried harder. I could have mended things between us if I knew time was running out. I was just so hurt."

"Of course you were. He made a spectacle out of you." Connie needed new support methods. "Now, you're going to put on a pretty dress and come out with Matt and me tonight for a nice supper. Sheryl wants the hours. I already gave her your shift."

"I don't drink, you know that, and I'm not coming along as a third wheel on your date night." Nothing was more embarrassing than being a single tag-a-long.

"Date night is tomorrow," Connie said. "There will be music. The band is nice, and you my dear need some music in your life.

Don't make me come over to that lodge and drag you into the car myself. Now go home and get some sleep, we will be there at eight."

"Bossy woman," Samantha said playfully before slipping out the door.

"Eight Sam, whether you're dressed in jeans or dress, you're going. I suggest a dress," Connie yelled behind her as the big door shut between them.

Sam climbed the stairs into a crisp Kentucky morning. A cloudless sky in robin egg blue was simply refreshing. Cold air slid over her cheeks, whipped her long blonde hair to the side, and kissed her good morning. It was a fine morning, she thought on a yawn.

As she made her way to the old Ford she and Nelly shared equally, Sam thought about her friend's offer. Maybe getting out would do her good. She could ready her son Brody for bed before leaving. Yes, it would be good to let her hair down with the crew, her police and responder family. But first, she had a handsome young man waiting to share Saturday morning breakfast with her and a pillow with her name on it.

CHAPTER TWO

Henry Quinn stomped his lace up boots against the concrete, dislodging any remaining evidence that just thirty minutes ago he was wading a soybean field, searching for an illegal kill that had been reported. Two hours of trekking and all he found was it was best not to trust Erma Maddox when she had her evening medication. As a Kentucky Wildlife officer half the job was spent answering calls that seldom resulted in an arrest.

Satisfied he wouldn't track mud through Darlene's establishment he pushed through the left red door and stepped into the Brick. A man could shoot pool, dance with a pretty girl, and get a rack of the best ribs this side of the Missouri, at the Brick.

At this hour both sides of the two-part establishment equally smelled of stale beer, cigarettes, and cheap perfume. Not uncommon on a Saturday night after ten, but at eight, Quinn figured half the town had come out for ribs and chatter. He walked towards the bar, nodding a few hello's along the way. Connie hadn't been subtle when mentioning David not handling his recent divorce well. Quinn knew a little about nursing a broken heart, and better yet, how to be a good friend. They were to meet on this side of the Brick where solitary men met.

At the bar, Quinn ordered a coke from the barely-legal-looking girl drenched in black from her long sleeves to her lipstick. Darlene must be desperate for help these days, he thought. He debated ordering her famous ribs. Those things were legendary and the sole purpose of the other side of the Brick being crowded seven days a week. Not a spare table was in sight in the dim lighted dining area. Soft music played on the jukebox, a country ballad that inspired a few couples to sway on the small dance floor towards the front.

Sipping his coke, Quinn surveyed the scene while he waited. Mack Dawson and Bob Cane sat at a four top table, splurging on the full rack for each of them. The two always hung out after work. If he hadn't tried and failed at baseball, perhaps he too, like the rest of the locals, would have joined the union over at the power plant. Quinn chased a dream, failed, and in the end lost everything.

He did love his job. Pay was horrible. Wardens made less than local law enforcement and yet covered larger regions, but he had few needs to finance a solitary life. But something about wearing the same uniform his father had, made him feel closer to the man he barely remembered.

At another red-clothed table, Quinn locked gazes with Eric Sutton. The local preacher had said the last words over every member of Quinn's family and the only time Quinn noted a hitch in his never-wavering tone was at Aaron's grave when they were finally allowed to bring his body home and plant him on the hill with the generations of Quinn's and Elliot's rested for that eternal rest. Nelly's youngest hadn't been overseas long when they got the news, and his dream of being a soldier ended almost before it began. Quinn lifted his coke in salute. The preacher nodded before focusing back on his chatty wife.

Quinn was blessed to have Nelly and Uncle Clayton take him in when he was six and orphaned. Being raised on an eight-hundred-acre tobacco and cattle farm with cousins that were more like siblings didn't erase all he lost when his parents died, but it had given him all the roots he would ever need in this life. Now forty, he was feeling the pressures. He had stalled setting down roots of his own, but no matter how close he came to trying, she held him back.

His silly boyhood infatuation was making him forever miserable, a self-inflected discontentment that he had the power to change and yet, wouldn't. He accepted that long ago, but lonely nights still tore at a man.

"Been waiting long?" David strolled up and took a stool beside him, jerking Quinn back to the present.

"Not really. Clark should be along soon. Nelly said he was having her old Ford taken to the garage. Apparently it broke down on Sam this morning coming off her shift" he said gruffly. It irked him to no end to be the last to know when help was needed.

"Mad she didn't call you, huh?" David motioned for the girl behind the bar. "I guess it's vacation time for her now, sort of," David chuckled and took a sip.

"Why those two insist on keeping that lodge running is beyond me. It took me three weeks to get a full day off just to clean the gutters so Sam wasn't up there doing it herself." Because Quinn knew she would at some point. Last summer she painted the barn roof without his knowledge. So he ramped up his evening visits, and made Nelly promise to call him over such duties next time.

Woman had grit, and was building quite the name for herself. Quinn had her website pinned on his phone to keep informed. September archery hunts. Trail cam pictures of velvety horns. Tons of reviews from happy hunters praising the Deer Creek Lodge, and if half of what Nelly rattled about was true, this upcoming hunt was going to pack the lodge for both solid weeks of the modern firearm season.

"Then stop sneaking around her shift schedule." David pinned him with a brow. "Don't you think it's time to get over that or do something about it? I swear you do things bass ackwards or not at all." Quinn looked over from under his black warden's cap.

"You know I can't," Quinn replied. David was there on the ball field over 20 years ago when the new blonde in town strode onto the field. His cousin Becky had an arm wrapped around her, introducing her to all her friends.

She looked like a high school junior with all that blonde hair and legs that stretched for miles. It was to Quinn's bitter disappointment to find out she was only in junior high. Samantha was twelve but shined and bloomed like the wildest first flowers of the mountain. More admiring than her looks was how easily she handled a half dozen high school boys flanking her as she crossed the field. She was a woman of control, even then.

When Becky introduced them, Quinn felt his heart do that little achy thing that hearts apparently do whether you are male or female. He'd offered her his hand and that was it; Quinn was lost to the new girl in town. The memory had not been lost to him. Quinn had never seen eyes so blue, a color of sophistication and confidence. She was a diamond dropped into the small town rough with a smile that could trip up a ball field full of boys.

His moral upbringing forced him to face the realities of it all. She was a child and he was looking at her like a woman. As months passed, she frequented the Quinn house. She and Becky were like peas of the same pod. The more she came, the more he knew they were a set, meant to find their way to each other in time. So time was what he hoped would pass quickly as he readied for college. She came to see him off that day as a nineteen-year-old boy left Milford for a career in baseball and a full scholarship. Quinn would never admit it, but that was his ten seconds, his moment, if God really did deliver such to boys, that he saw his future.

Instead, he bid her farewell, told her he hoped to see her soon, and walked away. She'd grow up while he was gone, and he would return with all intentions of winning her. If patience was a virtue, he had become its vice. Waiting turned out to be the worst decision of his life.

"She barely looks at me and I can't blame her after the way Dale treated her. I stop and see Brody. Kid's got me any time he needs me." Quinn shook his head. "Boy looks just like Aaron in one light, his momma in another." Quinn wondered if Nelly ever thought the same, looking at her grandson with so many of her youngest son's traits.

"I still think you were a chicken for not trying before the kid."

"She was a kid. I was seven years older than her, David. What father would have let me date his daughter at twelve? Ben may have been a bit wrapped up in his work and all, but he'd have noticed that and I would have on the other side of the law." Quinn added.

"Didn't stop the old fart from letting Dale have a shot at her," David added. No, it hadn't, Quinn set his jaw in the reminder of how many things his cousin got away with over the years.

"She practically lived at the house while I was gone. Bound to happen I guess. Dale was always charmed." Quinn swallowed the rest of his Coke which now tasted flat and bitter.

"Lucky is a better word." Quinn knew David wanted to say more about Dale, but respectfully let it go. No one liked to talk ill of the dead without fear of consequences.

"How was Sybil Spencer's daughter?" Quinn changed the subject.

"Not a scratch. I can't say the same about her Subaru. Do you listen in on all the calls, or just when certain people work dispatch?" David smarted.

"Part of the job," Quinn smirked. "She's good at it. I knew she would be." David agreed.

"She is better than those three Connie hired. We've done a lot of talking about Samantha Quinn over the years, you realize that?" He did, but before he could respond, he was summoned.

"Henry Quinn." Quinn winced at the sultry sound. He didn't bother to turn, hoping Felicity would get distracted. Her heavily floral scent arrived before the rest of her endowments did and Quinn fought off a sneeze. "I haven't seen you in here for a while handsome."

"We're having a boy's night," David added. "No girls allowed." Felicity waved a finger back and forth in front of him.

"No girls indeed," she purred like a cougar letting her fingers brush along Quinn's neckline. Quinn shrugged slowly and turned. Felicity was poison and that poison had no antidote.

"You going to buy a woman a drink?"

"No," Quinn said bluntly and turned back to the bar. The goth bartender smirked and shook her head. Even she knew Felicity Brown and her alluring charisma.

"Now David here on the other hand..." Quinn threw him under the bus, served him right for those earlier teases.

"No. No. I'm good. I'm good. Just because Chrystal left doesn't mean I don't still love my wife." Another reason Quinn had remained close friends with David after all these years. *What God brought together let no man separate.* Those words had haunted Quinn for a couple decades because Henry Quinn never dared taking on the big man upstairs.

Not one for being ignored, Felicity huffed and flung her hair behind her shoulder. "The band is good, how about a dance Quinn?"

"Not much for dancing. How about you drag Mack up there, might make his night." Quinn suggested, shooting David a sly grin.

"Oh, Mack Dawson is a looker," she said and slipped onto the stool next to him. "But he's too neat and picks at his food. Handsome as can be but in all the years he's lived here, I've never known him to date a single woman."

"Maybe he prefers keeping a low profile, and showering regularly," David mocked.

"Maybe, but something about him is a mystery, and oh look, another mystery." Felicity turned and anchored a long thin arm around Quinn's shoulders. That cheap floral scent was going to take two washings for him to get out. Why women drenched themselves was a wonder. "Thought she was too good for this place," she snarled. Quinn brushed her off and turned.

Matt Fleming, the local fire chief and Quinn's old batting mentor strode in dressed like Sunday church in his slacks and sweater, with his beautiful wife, Connie, on his arm. Matt could never have done better than winning that heart. And what a heart Connie had. She'd hired Sam without asking him any questions and took on Dale when he fought the whole idea of his wife working dispatch. Quinn knew what being a dispatcher meant to Sam. He knew what drove her to see no one ever slacked again in an emergency.

It was Sam who called 911 the night his cousin Becky was kidnapped. It was Sam who had license plate numbers and notes with all she noticed around her ready when the cops arrived. If the dispatcher that night hadn't thought it a prank, and hung up on Sam two times, Becky might still be here. The best way to fix a broken thing was to sometimes do the work yourself and she thought so too and had become what failed her back then. She was good at it too.

"What's she doing here?" Quinn muttered when Sam came into view.

"She needs heels. Poor little girl doesn't even know how to dress beyond jeans and pigtails," Felicity scoffed, but Quinn barely registered the words.

"Looks to me like somebody's ready to get back on the horse, and dressed like that she won't have any trouble. Connie deserves a medal." David said absentmindedly. Felicity was still muttering nonsense as Quinn slipped off the stool and got to his feet. Heads were turning and he was in no mood to deal with that. Samantha Quinn had no business here, dressed like that, smiling like that.

"She should be home with Brody. Heck it's almost nine on a Saturday, she should be working." He thought himself a quiet thinker with a level head. Right now, Quinn wasn't thinking level-headed at all.

"I told you she's on vacation," David said.

"You know what days she works?" Felicity interrupted, a bit of a whine in her pout. Still some insecurity there, Quinn noted from the woman who helped wreck Sam's world. Quinn narrowed his gaze. Sam didn't look like the grieving widow, a single mother, or one who worked two jobs.

She looked ravishing.

Even when the local band finally started to play, Quinn didn't hear sound. He only heard the ringing in his ears grow louder as his blood went from warm to a full boil as Ed Zimmerman's head shot up across the room and his gaze aimed right at her.

CHAPTER THREE

A s soon as the smoky air hit her, Sam sneezed. And that sneeze turned into another, then another. Why Darlene let people smoke in here was beyond her. No other public establishments allowed such, she fussed silently. She pasted on a weak smile against the mingling aromas. She couldn't let Connie think she was uncomfortable, overdressed, and out of her element. Socializing was overrated, but Connie seemed to be a pro as she chatted to everyone along the way to their table.

At forty-five, Connie was ageless. Raven black hair, only last year touched with color for the first time and jet-black eyes to match. Matt had married a true beauty queen. He knew it too, smiling proudly like he was with his bride on his arm. That one knew how to keep his lady happy.

The last time she stepped inside the Brick was her fifth wedding anniversary. Dale stood in the center of that floor wrapped around another woman, and her mad woman reaction was as subtle as a starving spider with a fresh victim. Sam had poured two glasses of the house beer over his head, slapped Marla Graber with an open palm, and stormed out letting them deal with all eyes on them in her wake. The locals dubbed the event 'The Sam dunk' just to be witty any time some poor woman stormed up a fit. It had become her yoke, having her name associated with tasteless behavior.

"Hey," Sam pivoted around to find Clark hurrying up behind her. He was out of breath and perspiring. "You clean up nice," Clark said playfully. He was used to seeing her in more casual wear and camouflage. Samantha suddenly felt self-conscience. The burgundy dress had been hanging in her closet collecting dust for two years and if she had known where Connie was taking her she would have never worn it. She was surprised it even fit.

"It's amazing what a bar of soap and a brush can do."

"You're the last person I suspected to see here tonight," Clark said with that handsome Quinn trademark smile, the kind that had a way of looking teasing and mocking in the same gesture. She was here for dinner that was all, maybe a dance with Matt if Connie enforced it, but that was it.

"And you," Sam added a stiff tone. "Pregnant wife at home and you are here for what, the BBQ?" She crossed both arms, eyeing him suspiciously. She could smell the scent of those slender cigars he liked to think no one was privy to. Little escaped wives, Sam knew, and she was surprised Bethany had never put an end to the horrid habit. Clark threw up both hands in defense.

"Meeting some friends, guy friends, and Beth *is* craving the BBQ, so don't 'Sam dunk' me alright. Every soul in Milford eats here, Sam." He nudged her shoulder playfully.

"Sorry," and she was. "I'm out of practice when it comes to being, *out.*" Clark laughed when she let out a huff. "Connie dragged me here and I'm regretting it," she muttered nervously.

"You shouldn't. It's about time you get out and mingle with the people you help save every day." Clark leaned in and one-arm hugged her. "Plus I think it's going to get pretty interesting this evening, now that *you're* here and all." When they pulled apart his face still held that snarky grin, only now it looked about to burst in laughter.

"I'm not here to entertain so wipe that smirk off your face." She stepped back, her foot bumping into something hard, upsetting her balance. Two hands gripped her upper arms firmly to keep her from spilling over. Sam wheeled around to find the hands attached to none other than Henry Quinn. He looked like someone just kicked a puppy, his dark onyx eyes narrowing. The man could square up with a drunken Marv Clemmons with a loaded gun, but had avoided her for almost as long as she had known him.

"Samantha," that low draw in his voice, rattled her momentarily. "What are you doing…in a bar?" She took a deep breath and clenched her hands into tight balls at her side. It was none of his business what she was doing. Heat bubbled in her throat but she was trained to deal with all matter of emergencies so calming her temper and her surprise that Henry Quinn had two words to fling her way, was essential.

For years Sam avoided any gossip about Milford's most sought after bachelor. If Henry was mentioned, she'd simply walk the other way. Dale had told her plenty about this particular cousin and she learned at the ripe old age of thirteen, he was not someone to be trusted.

Henry Robert Quinn had been her first crush, and the sole reason Dale spent more time away from home than in it. Worse, everyone liked him, driving her mad. If she had a kind thought in her head, she'd not spare it on him. Holidays she dealt with him, because that's what family did, dealt with each other. She knew he regularly visited Nelly on evenings she worked, and to her misfortune, Brody adored him.

Then there was work, forcing her deal with the only game warden in four counties. The dispatchers and police officers were a unit, a family of sorts. And no way about it, Sam couldn't shake him from either family unit. Thankfully he kept his head down, his sentences short, and his thoughts to himself.

Until now.

Struggling for composure she craned her neck to look up and match his glare. Those eyes were dark and slick just like the jagged stones that littered the creek behind her house. No other Quinn possessed them. It was those eyes that had made a little girl beg God to grow her up quick. His eyes always looked darker, a little more dangerous, lacking hints of yellows and greens that were part of the

Quinn gene pool. In uniform sporting a freshly trimmed beard, he looked too good to be true.

"It's a restaurant too," she said coldly, quickly gathering her wits about her. He tried on irritation but it faltered into a cheap smirk in the telltale corners of his mouth as his gaze swept over her. They crossed paths plenty over the years and here she was still flustered. For an instant, she wondered what he thought of her dress or how she had grown up from the girl he stared at all the time. *Don't be stupid.*

"Connie invited me for an evening out." She fought the urge to shove her fist on her hips as he perused her attire with a disappointing scowl. Well, she didn't look half bad no matter what he thought. She posed confidently.

"Connie?" He wouldn't dare treat Connie with such rudeness. "So you're here…" He studied her once more, "for the ribs?"

"And come morning I will be sitting next to Nelly and Brody in a church pew, guiltless. I'm not here for the same reasons you are," she smarted.

Her blonde hair, a few shades darker than the last time he had seen her, still hung well below her delicate shoulders. Her eyes were just as maddening blue as he knew them to be. Sam pinned him with a look that could both intimidate and dare equally.

"Which are?" He kept his tone even, but couldn't shake how bad he wanted to toss her over one shoulder in fireman fashion and drag her home before half the county could catch a glimpse of what he always knew to be the most beautiful creature in Kentucky.

"To do as you always do. And look, you're dressed in uniform." She brushed imaginary dirt from his breast pocket. "That should help in your newest conquest. Let's see. So who this month do I add to my nightly prayers?" She crossed her arms, those big blue eyes spanning the room, and her chin doing that lift that said pride still forged her. Her delusions of him tore at his gut.

If she only knew, he thought.

"You're here fishing so," she continued, tapping a long finger on the front of her full lips. Quinn closed his eyes and took two breaths. He had no one to blame but himself. Since he skipped out on her and Dale's wedding where he was to be the best man, and took two months before meeting Brody, his God son for the first time, he was, in her eyes, a man who didn't care about family.

What did he expect, never showing her a lick of attention? It didn't seem proper a year after the funeral to get closer to her when she was still raw with grief. At two years Quinn realized he had waited too long.

"I hear Laini is single. That one should be easy for you now that your looks are slipping."

"Slipping," he adjusted his cap and reined back a smile. From this vantage point Quinn couldn't help but admire the fieriness still in her. He liked the boots too, not those hunting, hiking lace ups he often noted sitting by the back door of the house.

"Your hair's receding," she tossed out the insult in the same sweet tone one dropped a compliment. "Oh look, Felicity is here. Of course she is, because permanent fixtures don't move."

Gritting his teeth, Quinn couldn't help but shut down her tirade. "Sam you're acting like a child and dressed like..." he had to stop her now that she was hitting his nerves directly. They had circled around each other for years. Him trying to determine if she was worth a kind word the way she spoke to him so harshly, her trying to decide if she should brain him with a stick. Why couldn't he just walk away, find someone without the temperament of a badger. One who could stop a man's heart with one little red dress. Apparently Quinn was in favor of self-torture.

"As always, talking to you is like spitting in the wind. Go home Samantha." This time he didn't care how it sounded. What he did care about was that Samantha was at the Brick and wearing a dress that in all fairness was simple. But with curves and legs and all that hair, it wasn't just the dress turning so many eyes her way.

"No," she shot back. "I'm afraid you don't have the authority, Warden. You're out of your jurisdiction"

"Sam," Connie interjected before any more barbs passed between them. She turned to him. "Heard you and the boys were meeting up tonight."

Heard? Being here had been Connie's idea.

"Connie, Matt." He tipped his hat but refused to retreat. It seemed the center of two opposing sides was the place to be. A bar on the right, a restaurant on the left, and Samantha Carver Quinn, smack dab in the middle just where he somehow always kept her.

"Thought it was date night," he shot Connie a this-is-not-acceptable look. She probably convinced Sam to wear that dress too.

"Quinn," Matt reached out a hand and Quinn shook it. "Two beautiful women, one for each arm," Matt boasted.

Mr. and Mrs. Florence strolled past. Mr. Florence sporting a nice shiner and everyone watched as they took a seat.

"Looks like they forgave each other," Connie chuckled. "The young can learn so much from the old, don't you think dear?" Matt shook his head though he didn't seem to know to what he was agreeing too.

"And how could we let this one, looking a pretty as she does, spend her Saturday night watching chic flicks and eating popcorn alone, again." Connie's brow raised to exclamation point the statement.

"Thirty-five and too beautiful to be wasting a night when she can be enjoying it with me," Connie jested and squeezed Sam affectionately.

"Thirty-two," both Quinn and Sam said at the same time. They locked glares again. For Pete's sake even her sharp glare yanked the strings holding his heart.

"I agree. Hi Sam," David reached out, took Sam's hand and gave her a twirl. His whistle only drew more attention and Quinn felt his collar tighten. Was everyone having a laugh at his expense tonight?

"If I didn't still love my wife, you'd be in trouble right now missy." Sam blushed but it quickly turned into a frown the second Felicity strolled up and looped her long arm into his.

"You promised me a dance cowboy," Felicity said, eyes smiling at Sam. Nothing about this night was turning out well. Just a drink with a friend had now turned into one hair short of a public scene.

"Well Deputy Schiffer," Sam said lifting her chin, "I think they are playing our song." With a smile and an extra sway in her hips, she drug poor David towards the dance floor. "Connie, order me a Dr. Pepper please, and a half rack. I'm going to go work up an appetite tonight," she called out over her shoulder. And she was gone, leaving Quinn in the awkward center of the circle between establishments while the faint scent of her taunted him in her wake.

"Felicity, let go of me," Quinn ordered. Two unladylike growls and he heard heels retreat behind him. He needed to get over this stupid infatuation that had followed him into manhood. A man couldn't go on pining for a life not his and she had clearly gotten over her infatuation twenty years ago. She hated him worse than she did persimmons.

It was time.

Time to let her go.

CHAPTER FOUR

Sam pulled her ponytail through the hole in the back of her pink camo cap. She set her pack filled with batteries, memory cards, and all the essentials required to tend to the northeastern side of the farm's wildlife cameras, into the four-wheeled side-by-side's seat. Climbing behind the wheel she shut the door. That upgrade had cost her two weeks salary but when temperatures dropped below freezing she couldn't call it a waste.

Turning the key, the engine rattled to a satisfying hum. Out the poly windshield the last golden leaf of autumn floated leisurely to join its comrades already waiting to be swallowed by winter's first run. It was nature, the living and the dying. From a budding birth to a shrinking decomposing death, everything recycled.

She was barely ten when her mother died, and she had learned of death's permanence. Unlike the child who clung desperately to hope and miracles, Sam saw it all more clearly now. Loving someone didn't protect them from uncertainty, and love was not always enough. Men sometimes fell to their deaths, best friends sometimes disappeared in the dark, and mothers sometimes died. It was fact. It did no good wasting time pondering on the things one couldn't change.

"A little extra prayer never hurts." That's what Nelly always preached. But prayers hadn't brought her mother back, and they hadn't held her marriage sound. Still, whatever life tossed her way she wouldn't be her father. She wouldn't run away from her troubles. Sam had stayed in her loveless marriage, dealt with the hand given her, because she promised she would. It had been the last promise she ever made.

Anger and guilt were odd bedfellows, and made for a miserable existence. She showed that off just last night. What was she thinking, scratching Quinn with all her claws? She couldn't blame him entirely, now could she?

Driving along the bumpy earth-packed road, Sam aimed for the meadow centering the farm. Seasons came and went, each having their own pleasures, their own magical moments, but that transition between fall and winter was her favorite. Sunlight blinked between the trees aligning the road to her left. Turkey tracks darted the muddy roadway ahead. This was her place, the quiet out here where thinking and worry could not enter. She obeyed nature's rules and thought only of the moment. Out here, she simply…existed.

She loved this farm and all it entailed. Mowing the fields, planting food plots, setting up cameras, and she did her diligence maintaining good buck profiles on her website. Hunters loved the big ones with fetching names like Zeus, Great 8, and Monarch. Brody loved thinking up the names too. Sam had to draw a line at such tags as Iron Man and Spider Man, but Hulk worked perfectly for a massive 16 pointer that was proving a legend. He was a skilled mature buck that had for three years eluded the broad head steel of the arrow and the lead and copper of a bullet. If early pictures where any indication, Sam was certain he would be the most sought-after buck again this year.

Nothing got a man's heart rate pounding faster than drop tines and a wide rack. Seven bucks this year looked to have strong trophy potential and her site was booming with comments to see more.

She parked the 900 Ranger side-by-side and shut the engine off. Hunters liked to think they were tough, rugged even, sitting in stands instead of stalking their prey, but she heard nothing but praise on cold five o'clock mornings when she drove them to their stands in the heated utility vehicle and even more praise at dusk when their cold bones had a warm ride back to the lodge.

Climbing out, she zipped up her camouflaged coat, tucked a few stray hairs under her cap, and shouldered her backpack. A stiff wind made of northern cold and a cloud-cluttered sky fingered her neck briskly. Fox Sparrows, Longspur, Warblers, and Winter Wrens darted in and out of the meadow's stiff grasses. An Eastern Phoebe who had decided to stick around, chirped in protest of her arrival, then disappeared again to search out more seeds.

Sam reached back, pulled the hood of her camo jacket out from under her pack, and covered her cap to keep the chill off. The air smelled of winter and it was closing in faster this year than the last few. Snow flurries were expected tomorrow, not uncommon for northern Kentucky, but felt early still.

Brody would be happy with hopes of sledding, she thought as she eyed the heavens. Early cold also increased the rut, the mating rituals that made strong sensible bucks, stupid and careless.

She let out a laugh. Men were like that too she figured. She might have overreacted last night but what made Quinn think he could simply order her about was beyond her. And why did it unnerve her that Henry Quinn looked good in a beard. He always had such a strong chin and jawline, a straight roman nose, and perfectly positioned ears. But this older Quinn hadn't aged or depleted, he had improved. Further proof life simply wasn't fair.

Hiking along the lower trails, she reached the first deer camera, pulled out the memory card, replaced the batteries, and tried not to think how easily Henry could distract her.

Naked trees moaned in the breeze and squirrels scurried to finishing storing their supplies. Her veins warmed as she trekked from the end of the thirty-acre meadow and followed the trail through the turkey pass.

She knew this mountain like the back of her hand. Every vein that opened and flowed freely into the valley creek beds, every Ash that looked ready to collapse in the bore beetle invasion, and every den of dank wet coyote that said she was fair to allow predators a place to live too when all other farms nearby had no such tolerance. She could kill for food, but sport had been Dale's thrill. The way Sam saw it, even coyotes needed to eat.

She finished changing out the batteries in three mini Cabela cameras along the field, and two more near hunting stands along the tried and true trail along the bottom. Adjusting her pack, she aimed for The Chairs and the ghost who awaited her there. It was steep terrain to the rock wall encasing the entire Quinn property but she had walked the old trail a hundred times and was barely winded. Her long legs that looked out of place on a stubby upper body had its uses.

Twenty minutes later she reached the peak of field stone laid decades before her time. A rustle, followed by a blow of warning over the other side of the mountain told she had disturbed a deer's slumbers. She smiled.

Thirty feet to her left, she looked up and spotted the one-seater hunting stand, shingled in cedar and framed in oak. It grew out of the tree line and had a perfect view of the vast spring lake below surround by withering alfalfa. She tested the man-made wooden ladder rungs, mentally noted a weak one, and began to climb. No one hunted here. Not anymore. Once on top, she sat on the old bench made by her father-in-law, Clayton Quinn's own hands, and pulled out her water bottle.

Sam cleared her throat as she always did before speaking. "Brody's gonna be a pilgrim for the play this year. Your mother," she smiled, "she is determined to sew his costume, but you know how your mother is about doing things herself."

Maybe she was an oddity, talking to the dead, but who else could she share her day with? It only seemed right to talk to him about Brody, and to talk to him here. It's where Dale took his last breath. She owed him something, she knew. If she had been a better wife, maybe tried harder, he might not have felt the need to wander woods and women so easily. If she had tried harder, he would have loved her.

Sometimes when she talked about life, it wasn't Dale she felt listening. She didn't feel him down there or up here. He had never liked hearing about her day. That had to be the reason, she figured. No matter, she talked anyway, because the mountain did. The mountain listened.

Glancing down, just below, she thought of him. Dale was a lot of things, but clumsy Sam would have never called him. Yet he had been according to Ron Culver, the town's sheriff, and Casey McCloud, the local coroner.

Dale had leaned his rifle against this very tree. Why, when he had a strap to keep it shouldered? And what caused the 30-30 to fall at just the right moment, firing without a finger on the trigger at that exact second, was beyond them all. It wasn't an uncommon story. Hunting accidents happened. But for Dale, a man who taught safety, who trained others with firearms every other weekend, that part never settled with her.

Who was she to question death? When it made a decision, death didn't change its mind.

Sam closed her eyes and sighed heavily. Perhaps she would never know how she became a widow. Pushing all despairing thoughts aside, she focused on the living.

The mountain. It breathed, birthed, and never left.

A glint of white standing out among earthy hues caught her gaze. Tilting her head, Sam tried to decipher its origins. Antler sheds weren't to be found for another four months, but like the first time Dale brought her to hunt ginseng on this mountain and it's steep southern hillsides, Sam knew more than man hunted these hills. She still had the picture hanging on the wall of the bones they found that year. A bear, Quinn confirmed without a doubt. The front paw of it, at least. At barely twenty, the thought of bears at her back door scared her to death. Now at thirty-two, she would be thrilled if one would cross her stand view, grant her a smile in passing. She tapped her side, the holstered 38 Nelly insisted she carry along any time she wandered alone, just in case miracles happened and bears could smile.

Curiosity driven, Sam climbed back down, circled around what she considered holy ground, and wandered over the hill to investigate further. She scooted down the steep embankment on her rear and found the bone rather quickly. It lay left of a huge cherry. The tree's unnatural girth and purplish rigid bark glistened for a second when the sun found a hole to stretch its fingers out of the clouds.

Bending, she plucked the bone out of a layer of autumn leaves. Long and narrow, with evidence some young coyote pup cut his baby teeth here, or more likely a squirrel. They were notorious for scarring spring antler sheds if you didn't find them quick enough.

Turning the bone over and over only made her more curious, puzzled even. It was no animal she could think of. She had discarded her share of deer carcasses for the wild to recycle and only a deer would possess such a lengthy skeletal member. There had to be more, she told herself kicking up leaves about her.

"Well. You just dropped from the sky I guess," she jested. "I bet you have a good story to tell," she added. She could take it back, do an internet search. No way would she dare ask Henry.

Taking a step back for one last look of the area a loud crack echoed into the air, traveled down the hill and disappeared in the field and ponds below. Sam gasped as she recognized the sound of splitting wood. Seconds, that's all it would take to make Brody an orphan.

Legs straddled in an awkward half step, breath held, she looked down just as the earth opened its door and let her in. Grappling replaced a scream and the dark consumed her just before a wave of pain crashed over her.

CHAPTER FIVE

T he Everett Brothers had a habit that needed amended. Quinn had ticketed them, arrested them, and on a few occasions, went to blows with Roger, the eldest with a shorter fuse. Today, still raw over last night, he was in no mood to deal with the local deer poachers any longer. Some men took to learning a lesson like a cat to a bath. Knowing the tip called in this morning held merit, Quinn called David to meet him at the end of the Everett drive. Having a deputy in these cases was necessary. It was less than a week until modern firearm season, and that always brought out the restless ones.

"It looks like they're both home. That's Chris' car over there," David said through his rolled down window. "Who reported it?"

"Old man Watson said he woke in the middle of the night, saw Roger's truck, heard the shot. Let's do this right. I've been too kind to these two over the years. It ends today." Quinn said firmly.

"I'm good with getting backwoods boozers out of Milford," David said. "Let's get this over with. I haven't had my lunch yet." Quinn rolled up his passenger side window. Putting the truck in drive he proceeded forward with an extra caution. Being vigilant around these two meant survival. One never knew how Roger would react to law enforcement pulling up uninvited.

The single wide trailer sat center of the grass-less property. There was no under skirting to secure the outside elements from getting in and a front porch constructed out of wooden pallets stacked on top of each other. At least it looked level, Quinn thought as he brought his truck to a stop. Roger Everett stepped out before Quinn could put his truck in park and exit it. He knew why Quinn was there. That cocky grin said he wasn't coming easy either.

"Morning, Warden. Nice you could pay a visit, but a bit over-dressed aren't ya?" Roger lit a cigarette, coolly drawled. His hollow cheeks sunk inward indicating a few missing back teeth.

"It's past noon and you know exactly why I'm here Roger." Quinn stepped up to the porch as the deputy exited the car. Roger narrowed his gaze, took another draw of his cigarette and smiled.

"Brought help? Worried?" He hiked a clever brow.

"Do I look worried?" Quinn lifted the search warrant. "Chris needs to come out of the house. Is anyone else here?"

"Yeah, got a couple super models hog tied in the back," Roger laughed and yelled for his brother. Roger Everett was a good six foot, hundred-and-eighty-pounds of hot-headed lawlessness. But Chris, blonde haired, blue eyed, made his elder look like a tic tac in a bowl of oranges. The pallet porch dipped as Chris ducked through the doorway and stepped out of the trailer. Quinn didn't rattle as Roger had hoped. Big and dumb wasn't always an issue, so Quinn's focus remained on Roger, the more unpredictable of the two.

"You two been hunting lately?" David asked.

"Not season yet deputy." Roger replied. Quinn noted the sleeve of his blue jean jacket. From this angle, it looked like dried blood. Even his jeans speckled of evidence. This was going to be Roger Everett's last kill.

"Well we got a warrant to search the property. You two boys step on down here so we can do our jobs and get this over with."

"Can't go rummaging through a man's things just like that," Roger defended.

"This here," Quinn waved the warrant in the air, "says we can. Step on down now like the deputy asked." Quinn watched the two sulk and stomp down the stacked concrete block steps. "Over here. For our safety we have to ask if you have any weapons on you, or anything that can be used as weapon?" Neither man answered. "You are not under arrest, but considering your record, we are securing you for our safety. Do you understand," Quinn pulled two ties from his belt.

"You're not putting those on me, Quinn." Roger snarled, flicking his cigarette at Quinn's pant leg.

"I'm not searching this place with you at my back either. Cooperate, or I will just have the deputy arrest you now. If you haven't done anything Roger, this will be over and you can get back to your busy day." Quinn stepped forward. They stood toe to toe, neither backing down. "Turn around," Quinn ordered. Part of him hoped they cooperated, no surprises that would get one of them hurt. Part of him wanted a tussle, something to take his frustrations out on. Roger Everett was always a good tussle.

"Boys, you're no strangers to the process. Don't make this harder than it needs to be." David craned his neck to look up to Chris whose tousled hair looked like had he just rolled out of bed.

"We ain't making your job easy for ya," Roger quipped seconds before taking his first swing. Quinn anticipated the resistance and countered appropriately. Gripping Roger's arm, Quinn attempted to spin him, wrestle him to the ground, and do a quick capture of his hands behind his back. Only his old fellow classmate, former running back for the Panthers and the sole reason they won state three years straight, proved a challenge.

"Don't think too hard now Chris. Just put those tree trunk arms up and turn around," David ordered beside him, but Quinn couldn't think about David and the sleepy mountain right now as Roger reached for Quinn's gun. Quinn gripped his wrist with both hands while Roger pounded two hard blows with his other hand into Quinn's face. In one quick sweep of the leg, Quinn had the temperamental man off balance and wrestled him to the ground. Fists swung and curses crossed paths as Quinn twisted Roger's wrist hard enough he was sure the man cried uncle. It was endurance that won, and Quinn was glad he spent those extra hours running as he did. As he gathered Roger's hands and pulled another zip tie from his belt, Quinn looked up to two sets of amused eyes looking at him.

"My guy came peaceful," David shrugged, pointing a thumb towards the giant beside him. "Come on big boy," David said escorting Chris Everett to the back seat of his patrol car.

"Figures," Quinn growled, breathing heavily. "You always were a pain in the rear Roger."

"And you always could take a punch," Roger chuckled despite knowing he was defeated. "You know I owe ya one now Quinn. You should know better than come knocking on a man's door without being invited."

At the sound of his cell phone ringing, Quinn ignored Roger's weak threat. He placed a knee in Roger's back and pulled his phone out, surprised the screen wasn't shattered into a hundred pieces.

"Henry Quinn."

"Henry, its Connie." She seldom used his first name and never when calling him when he was on a job.

"I really can't talk right now Connie. If this was about the Brick last night, I'm not apologizing. And I know you did that on purpose." Maybe he did talk about Sam too much with her.

"No Quinn, I didn't think you would. I'm calling because," she paused, took a long inhale. "We had a call come in. I think you should head home," Quinn froze.

"What call?" Quinn let loose of his capture and got to his feet.

"It's not Nelly or Brody. Nelly called it in. It may be nothing." If it was nothing, Connie wouldn't have bothered calling and if Nelly and Brody were fine, that meant...

"Connie just say it. Why did Aunt Nell call 911?" Quinn looked over and met David's concerned look.

"Sam went out to check cameras early this morning and hasn't returned. Nelly thought she was just lingering, but at this point she was worried enough to call it in. I told her I would contact you. She is pretty upset." So was Connie by the sounds of her. His gut twisted tighter. Sam was...predictable.

"How long has she been missing?" Hearing part of the conversation, David quickly bent down to get his hands on Roger, freeing Quinn to deal with the call.

"No time on that. We know nothing Quinn. I..." Connie rarely choked on the job. It was only when one of their own was in need of help that birthed uncertainty. He shot a panicked glance towards the deputy.

"I got this brother, go on," David offered. Quinn was crossed between two responsibilities, but the decision came easily.

"I'm on my way. Who did you send out?" Quinn tapped David's shoulder and sprinted to his truck.

"Everyone Quinn. I even sent Matt and the boys from the fire department." Good girl, Quinn thought. "Ron is waking Clark now, and some of your aunt's neighbors have already been out looking." It *was* serious. Connie had downplayed that earlier. He accelerated out of the Everett's drive, leaving David to tend to the brothers on his own now that they were safely secured. Connie had sent everyone. For someone who was so cool headed that alone sent a fear marrow-deep into his bones.

Quinn reached the house in record time and barged inside to find Nelly sitting at the kitchen table with her cordless phone in one hand, her head in the other. "I probably shouldn't have called. She might just be hiking and enjoying herself. She hates when I make a fuss, but she is just never this late." Nelly choked back her emotions but he could see the mother who had buried her children fearing she might have just lost another.

"She has no business doing this alone. You did the right thing." Quinn couldn't hide his fury. "What time did she take out? And did she mention where she was even going? Did she take the pistol I gave you?" His mind was working overtime. A glance at the back-door said she had her waterproof boots on, but her heavy jacket still hung on the hook above. Quinn noted the long cylinder flashlight. It was November and it would be dark soon, especially with the clouds moving in.

Nelly got to her feet. "Calm down son. Sam is a smart girl," Nelly tried to soothe him. She often called him son, and he never minded one bit. In fact, Nelly was like a mother, his as well as his cousins, and her fretful expression and trembling lips reminded him of the way she looked the last time death took someone from her. Quinn took a deep breath.

"We can't both over-react here. One of us needs to stay levelheaded." Nelly shook her head. She was right. He needed to be strong, professional. Mighty hard to do when it was Sam in trouble.

"Sam would never miss getting back in time to pick up Brody from school, that's why I called the sheriff's office. She has the pistol, her backpack, batteries, memory cards, and water. I know she has her camo coat, the thin one," Nelly winced. "She wore jeans, those old boots of hers." Nelly was thinking of the cold too. "She drove the new ranger, but we found it in the meadow. I drove out there with Martin from next door. We didn't see anything. I yelled and yelled," Nelly took a breath.

"That's why I won't calm down," Quinn snapped a little harshly and stormed back to the front door as the sound of vehicles raced up. Time was wasting and for every minute wasted, Sam needed him.

"Sam is smarter than that. There are more than twenty sinkholes around here, and those are the ones I know about from ten years ago." He ran a hand through his hair, fisting his cap with the other. He had avoided Bear Claw Mountain for years. He didn't care much for hunting animals.

"She has stands, blinds, three ponds, and fifty trails. She could have…" Quinn couldn't finish one scenario of what fate could have come to Sam. There were too many.

"Stop that," Nelly ordered sharply. "Sam needs you to do what you were born to do. Protect and save. Let me be the worrier here. Sheriff Culver is calling in search and rescue. He swears by those dogs, and all the neighbors are coming too. I collected a few things like he asked and I called everyone I could get a hold of just before you walked in." She took a shaky breath and went to the sink. Wetting a long length of a dish towel, she placed it on his face. He had nearly forgotten just a few minutes ago he and Roger were beating the snot out of one another.

He took the towel and continued giving himself a quick cleaning. His field uniform looked as if he had been cave diving.

"I need to go pick up Brody from school before word gets out," she said with fresh worry and reached for her coat. Quinn's head fell. He took hold of the hallway chair back, meant for sitting and removing mucky boots or lacing them, and gripped hard. Something had to hurt, had to feel as he was feeling inside.

"Don't bring Brody back here. Not yet." She clenched his arm but to look at her might undo him. "Go for ice cream and visit Stella or something. Don't bring him here, to all of this. Sam wouldn't want that." A parade of flashing emergency lights and vehicles in every direction began filling up the driveway.

"I won't. You get on out there. Ron needs you today and you need the sheriff. Go find her Henry." With that stern order Quinn's head lifted and jaw tightened. He let loose of the chair and straightened his shoulders. This is what he did, combed the wilderness, protected and saved. Sam needed his years of training and experience and if he did find her, she would be furious.

Quinn inhaled, giving his loaded belt a once over just as an old truck raced up the drive. Temperatures were still holding around fifty, but tonight, frost was predicted to roll in thick and lay heavy into the late morning, or possibly snow making its first appearance. Wherever Sam was, she was cold and that wouldn't do.

Quinn didn't need to wait for the driver to exit the truck. He knew Ben Carver's vehicle well enough. Sam's dad had owned it for as long as Quinn remembered. The tall slightly bent man normally would be clocking into to work at this hour. Small town gossip ran faster than the Licking River rose in spring. Of course he would come, his daughter needed him. Ben might have shirked a few fatherly duties after losing a wife and moving to a new town with a teenager, but when it mattered, when it was important, he was always there.

"Be gentle. That man's lost a lot." Nelly muttered slipping into her coat and sidling up beside him.

"He isn't the only one," Quinn locked gazes with Nelly.

"No, I guess he isn't, but she is all he has." Nell said shouldering her purse. "Are there any rules against me taking your truck? Mine's in the shop." Quinn tossed her the keys and stepped off the porch to meet Ben.

"They said Sam was missing and by the looks of it, they were right." Ben said in a rusty, rattled breath. Outwardly he looked calm. Unlike Quinn, Ben was good at hiding how his gut twisted.

"Nelly called it in when she didn't return from checking cameras."

"Those stupid cameras," Ben growled taking up beside him as they marched towards the sheriff's car. Ron and his young deputy were both head down over a large map. Clark pulled up next. Exiting his truck, he was still dress in slacks from his insurance job.

The wide circle drive had become mayhem. Fifteen vehicles were flooding the yard on both sides of the house and more were pulling in by the minute. At least everyone had the common sense not to block the drive.

"Is this true?" Clark asked.

"Yes. We need you to take us through her routine. Nelly called a few neighbors when she didn't return. She even took one of the side by sides out. They didn't find anything but the Ranger parked at the northern end of the meadow.

"She swapped batteries and memory cards from the west side the day before yesterday. She could be anywhere from the Bear Wallow to The Chairs." Clark ran his hands through his dark hair. "She said she was behind. I knew we were behind," Clark said between gritted teeth. "We planned to be finished by today. I was supposed to help," Clark's voice hitched. "I had a claim to do and paperwork." Quinn gripped his shoulder.

"You can't be everywhere," Quinn said. He was thankful Clark helped as much as he did. "*We* need you now. You're the best chance she's got since you know her routine." The three reached the sheriff and his deputy, looking perplexed at the lay of the farm now sprawled out over the hood.

"David has your boys locked up. Found enough evidence to hold them, but I told him to put them on ice for now. Pete is keeping an eye on them downstairs." Quinn nodded to the sheriff, confident the retired jailer still capable, and glanced at the map.

"Geez Quinn this place is bigger than I thought. I think we need more volunteers." Ron Culver had been sheriff of Milford since Quinn accepted a scholarship to play baseball. He was bald now, and his common humor and old school shirt was now looking lost and a bit sweaty.

"Clark here can help with that." Quinn added. Clark stepped forward and turned the map to suit him.

"She was checking cameras around the farm and meadows to send the pictures to clients and post on the lodge's site. I know she has covered this area." He pointed to the lower end of the property line before sliding it south. "We did this section yesterday." Quinn re-familiarized himself with the layout, the terrain. Clayton had once taught him every deer trail and sink hole there was.

"What about the cemetery? Isn't that where you plant beets and turnips for those stands? There's two old wells back there." Quinn muttered the last sentence and took a breath. The thought that Sam could have fallen into one of those old wells made his stomach curl.

"Yeah, but I did those, that's another reason why I was late Saturday meeting you and David at the Brick. If Nelly and everyone looked already, I say the meadow is out. Nelly would have been thorough." Clark locked eyes with Quinn. "And the two wells are filled with rock now. Sam had worried about that and had that done about four years ago. Anyone got a pen?"

The sheriff produced a pen from his left shirt pocket. "If we have more volunteers, send them over these areas." Clark made to big circles around the areas surrounding the meadow. "Now where was the side-by-side found," Clark asked and Quinn pointed to the map.

"She could be up at the wallow, maybe following the trail along the wall." There were at least a dozen trails branching off of that though. Ben was apparently more involved with his daughter's comings and goings than in the past. If only Quinn had been. He swallowed back the regret of remaining at arm's length all these years, out of respect.

"I can mark all the cameras and stands from there to The Chairs, but it's Sam." Clark shrugged. "She likes the hiking, that's why she left the Ranger. Quinn, she could be anywhere." They locked eyes again, silently reading the severity of the situation without saying it.

"I know this trail well enough to go alone," Ben said. "Sam puts me there during bow season every year."

"I can take the four-wheeler up to the wallow and see if I pick up a trail there," Clark added.

"When are the dogs going to be here?" Quinn spoke to the sheriff.

"I think that's them now," Ron said as two trucks with silver boxes in the back-slid into the drive.

"We can do three teams for the area we suspect as the hot zone, see if the dogs pick up on something. Volunteers can comb the bottoms and these places Clark here feels have already been gone over. People miss things when they worry." Quinn agreed with the sheriff. The dogs were already sounding, eager to get to work and Quinn was ready right along with them. Time was waning. An afternoon chill blew in, gusting in sporadic breaths and she was out there, somewhere waiting.

CHAPTER SIX

After everyone was briefed and a quick lesson in search and rescue was given to volunteers, the mission began moving ahead. The dogs picked up Sam's scent rather quickly. Quinn was saddled with Clay Jamison and his redbone Merle while Clark and Ben led another team northeast. For two hours Clay marked hot spots Merle signaled at. Quinn hoped the dog wasn't following Sam's trail from the day before. Trust, his conscience whispered. He had to trust a four-legged critter with Sam's rescue. Needing more assurances, Quinn shot up a prayer for the dog, for Sam, and for trust. He'd put his trust in the Almighty.

They climbed hills, followed hollers, and trekked through creek bottoms. "She covers a lot of ground," Clayton clipped out as they crossed another dip between hills. The woman was everywhere. That would have made Quinn smile any other day. It was another reason he had always loved her, that stamina and love of nature she possessed.

The demands of searching for the lost required stamina and as Clay's breath heaved, Quinn hoped the man didn't hinder the search. Quinn's job required one to keep his body physically in tune. Climbing hills was part of his job description. Clay was younger, but his duties at the local mill didn't require endurance.

When they reached the bottom of Turkey Pass, Quinn raised his eyes to the darkening mountain, a fading sun winking its final glint beside him. He hadn't climbed that peak or touched this side of the farm in nearly six years. A shiver ran over him and the chilling wind had nothing to do with it. The Chairs rested up there, on that narrow point facing the sunset. Three large boulders sitting side by side, shaded in the summer months by a few large oaks leaning into the sun's path.

It was a place for thinking, watching sunsets, and held a grand view of the lower valley. As a boy it was his favorite place to come to and ponder life's mysteries, telling God your thoughts without anyone listening. He felt his father there. If he had lived, dad would have found the spot a favorite too. Now it was a place of sadness and nothing could force him to go up there, the place Dale breathed his last breath.

God disagreed.

Merle's long auburn ears perked and then flapped as he let out three long deep-throated barks. "He's got something." Clay flipped on his headlamp and Quinn pulled his light from his service belt and began scattering the ground with light.

"You can see where someone dug in here. Small print too," Clay pointed. Quinn walked forward, noted the disturbed earth, the scatter of leaves, and the deep cut where boots clung for traction. Alarm bolted through him.

"Guess we're climbing," Clay said, unsnapping Merle's leash and signaling him forward. Quinn closed his eyes, let out a long exhale, and then dug in behind Clayton straight to the top.

She was cold and everything hurt like the dickens. With a deep, icy moan Sam tried moving her limbs only to shrivel back with a soundless cry. Death couldn't hurt this bad, she reasoned, trying her best not to shiver. It only made the pain in her leg hurt worse and no doubt about it, her head had taken the brunt of whatever hit her.

The air was thick, uncommonly damp. Was it night? Fear gripped at her throat in a fresh wave of panic. How long had she been here, wherever here was?

Her nostrils burned, but she didn't have the strength to open her mouth and try living that route. Her senses weren't that hindered for her to forget the moments just before the world snapped shut.

The bone, the sound of wood splintering, and then the fall.

Had she dropped into a sinkhole or some old forgotten cellar? Up this high, steep terrain, she thought not. It hurt to think, so she stopped torturing herself by doing it. She was fading again, but she wasn't dead. Too cold to be dead, but death was certainly toying with her.

"Lord, please don't make my baby an orphan," she begged, hoping God would deliver her back to her son. "He's lost so much." Crying took effort and she hadn't any left. Still, Sam was determined to find her way out, back to Brody.

Digging in her pocket, she found the side-by-side keys and flicked on the little pen light that was attached. She fisted the earth on the next wave of pain. Acorn shells dug into her palms before crumbling. She was drifting out of consciousness again. She fought for awareness. Clearly she was going to die because death stood not more than four feet away, waiting for her. Suddenly the next wave of nothing took her.

Dogs.

Sam was certain she could hear them. That long signaling howl to say they treed a coon. Lights flickered on the outside of her eyelids. She shook so hard she figured she was imagining it all until she felt her head lift. It was so slight, like a soft cradle, but she was certain it was being lifted.

"Oh God thank you," a voice spoke, hollow and distant. "I've got you baby. You just hold on now," it continued. It sounded like dad, but how could the living speak to the dead?

So, not dead, but not fully alive either.

Something warm brushed her cheeks, her forehead. So very warm. She was dreaming. Dreaming of a time when her father would kiss her goodnight, tuck her warm and snuggly into bed. But he sounded afraid and anxious. Two things her impassive father hadn't been since her childhood days.

"Send down the basket and call in medical and transport!" She flinched, sending a jolt of lightening through her body. She was aware something very real was happening around her. Her head pounded. Her knee and shoulder felt like they were no longer attached properly. Shattered, she felt shattered and someone was here with her here in this dark cold place to help gather the pieces. She should have known the guys would come. They were a family, watched over her like brothers. Of course they came. But which of them was it, holding her hand just now?

"Drop me a blanket David, and get Ben up here." In his desperate tone, recognition came. Suddenly she no longer wanted to dream or go dark, but live. She tried moving again.

"Calm down Sam, I've got you sweetheart." *Sweetheart.* Sam tried forcing her eyes open as she felt something warm and light fall over her. She had been gripping something. The bone, now she remembered the stupid mystery that got her into this mess in the first place.

Henry's fingers pried her stiff cold finger apart and relieved her of it. She preferred the heat of that warm hand and didn't resist, but clung to it, gripping to it desperately. She could regret it later; right now, she needed him and his skills to get her back to her son.

"I'm covering you up and I have to move you into a basket so we can get you out of here."

"Brody," she mumbled the barely audible words. Weight laid on her shoulder. *A blanket.* Hair brushed her cheek as his body quivered in rhythm with her own. It was his forehead touching her.

So warm against her Sam wished she could get closer, steal some of what he had.

"He's waiting for his momma," the voice broke as warmth began fighting for her. Heroes weren't supposed to cry but Sam was certain this one did. Her eyelids fluttered open to the shadows and a frail stream of light. Brody was waiting for her and Henry was beside her.

"Henry," she whispered as she felt herself fading again. "It had to be you."

His heart thought it couldn't take another pounding, but sure enough that muscle was working overtime today. Her voice was raspy, weak, and she shook so hard he feared she was becoming hypothermic.

"We're all out of white knights I'm afraid," he teased and brushed his face in case she noticed how just the sight of her gored his steady emotions. "Sorry to disappoint your memorable rescue my dear," he added, relieved she was still with him. No witty comeback met him but a grin tried to respond on her quivering lips. That was a good sign. If she rose up and started yelling at him, he would be even more thankful.

He shifted his flashlight. Blood had pooled from the side of her head at some point, but now it was dark and gelled. Quinn noted the long thick sliver of wood piercing her upper left arm and clenched his teeth. She hadn't lost much blood, he deduced, not as cold as she was. She had fallen more than a dozen feet through an old wooden roof or floor of some sort. He left the splinter in place for a professional but the urge to take it away was present.

"You fell darling. Your head is bleeding and there is something sticking out of your arm." They were professionals, and it was always best to state the obvious so she wouldn't overreact once her mind and body connected. Quinn had no idea how long she had been down here, how severe her injuries truly were, but for now he thanked God he found her.

"Thank you for helping us find her," he said. "Does anything else hurt?" He scanned the light over her.

"Everything," she said between chattering teeth as he removed her firearm, set it aside.

"They are going to lower a basket any minute. I have to move you into it so they can pull you up. Do you understand, Samantha?" She mouthed a soundless yes. The urge to kiss her had never been greater. To cradle her to his chest was overruled by safety.

He had let her go once, hoping she would be there when he returned. Then he had to watch for years as life treated her unfairly. Looking at her now, he wouldn't make that mistake again. David was right. He had been a coward. Doing the right thing hadn't been right at all. Dale was gone, and Sam was alone. If God got her out of here safely he would do what he should have done years ago. Win her heart. She already had his.

Spinning the light around, he investigated the dark lay of the crevasse to see if it was man-made or nature's own trap. Voices above announced EMS was topping the hill. An earthy wall of smooth clay forged in slight rises and dips to his front cast eerie shadows in the light. Planks and old pole beams said Sam wasn't the first to be here, wherever here was. Squinting against the play of shadows between two wooden beams, Quinn's breath caught and the light froze still.

Two long narrow shapes, dark and earthy, held a vaguely familiar profile in the back of his mind. As he lifted the beam of light higher, the sight of Barney, his junior high health class mascot, came into full view. Two fibulas, two femurs, rose to a butterfly pelvis sunken into the soil. He blinked, hoping his imagination had just decided to take over a brain worn with the urgency of finding Sam, but ribs protruding out of earth slayed that theory fast as his light rose to a skull and hollowed eyes tilted down facing them. This was no replica. This was very real.

When she moaned, Henry wrenched the light away to conceal the skeleton quickly. He cradled her cheek. Spoke softly so she knew he was still with her until she faded out again. Surely what had caught his eye had been some teenage prank long forgot about.

Cautiously he got to his feet, investigated further and found it was a soul, lost and buried, until now. Curiosity sparked, he floated the light around, noting ghostly roots from the large cherry above, a web, dangling and stretching for a stronghold. It was a natural hole made by time and gravity under the massive cherry, but someone had taken the time to nurture it into something else.

The hairs on the back of his neck bristled as he followed the roots to a wide opening. He shifted for a better view. Insects littered the floors. Their hard shells crunched under foot when he stood.

He hadn't noticed it when he was lowered down here, but now the sound was spine-chilling and enhanced the scene.

Four steps were all it took to stand in a wooden secured passageway of discovery and a place where real nightmares came to life.

Ducking, he peered inside. "Oh Lord," he said in response. The human body has a total of two-hundred-and-seventy bones in the beginning of their life. By adulthood that number decreases to two-hundred-and-six. And by Quinn's utterly dazed and stunned math skills, there was a village before him.

Wooden boxes were in the rounded corners, overflowing with their ivory treasures. In the earthy walls between unmeasured wooden supports, hollowed eyes looked towards a rickety folding chair in the center of the low-ceiling room. A lamp sat on the chair waiting to be lit as if someone wanted to see what was displayed here. From pearly white against his straight Eveready flashlight beam, to the dark shadows bouncing against his shaking hand, bones and faceless souls filled the room.

The bone he took from Sam's cold grip played a part. That one bone had distracted her from coming home. One soul had reached out hoping to be found and now Sam had found them all.

"Lord what have you dropped her into," he murmured in a dazed and disturbed voice.

"Quinn!" A voice yelled from up top, filling the lost chamber, and Quinn jerked as it brought him back to the situation at hand. Getting Sam and himself out of this place had never been more urgent. "Basket's coming down!" Quinn shook his head in slow movements as the scene before him burned into his mind.

"Henry," the soft voice broke the spell that held him and he hurried back to her side. Kneeling on the littered earth beside her, he collected his breath in case she noticed. There was no danger behind him, yet positioning himself between her and that tomb of the dead was necessary. He couldn't chance Sam seeing. Heck, he didn't want to see it. First save Sam, get her to help. Then Quinn would deal with whatever horror they had stumbled upon.

Bright lights quickly flooded the room as volunteers gathered overhead. "I'm here darling. They are lowering the basket. I'm going to cover your face to protect you from debris." A lie that was, a quick decision to prevent her from more trauma. Quinn wasn't sure he had his head wrapped around what his eyes had seen just yet.

"Just close your eyes, it's all about over."

"I thought I was dead," she said weakly. "Thought he had come for me." Her words sickened him, but Quinn wasn't about to tell her how right she nearly was.

"Your father is waiting for you. Brody is out eating ice cream with Nelly and hasn't a clue." That was what Sam needed to hear. Carefully, he lifted her and laid her into the basket. When she groaned against the exchange he hoped he hadn't caused her more pain. His thumb brushed her cheek as those dark eyes glistened in the light at him until he covered them and the basket was lifted to the fold of those who awaited to care for her.

CHAPTER SEVEN

Quinn removed his hat and took a deep breath. The last twenty-four hours had been a roller coaster. He had yet to make it out to the Everett place to collect evidence and secure a good case against the brothers. They were the least of his concerns currently. From the time the call came in that Sam was missing, until he had to take Sheriff Culver back into the hole, the roller coaster plunged and twisted and sped in a hazy blur.

He should have showered, changed into fresh clothes before coming here to the hospital. His knees were soiled with clay, now dried greyish blue over the regulation subdued forest green. Quinn had to see her, know for certain Connie wasn't making things sound better than they really were. He turned the corner to the short hall that held room number 216 just as Ben stepped out holding the tan hospital water pitcher, rippled bendy straw included.

"Hey," Ben greeted looking up. "Thought she might need this freshened up for when she wakes again."

"How's she doing?" Quinn neared. Ben's eyes took him in, noting Quinn's disheveled state.

"Better than you by the looks of ya. My girl do that to ya?" Ben pointed to Quinn's face, the bruises he had there.

"Had a tussle before..." *Before your girl scared the life out of me.* Ben grunted. It was his signature reply when words didn't do the job.

"Doc said she can go home in the morning. They did another scan and there isn't any swelling on the brain. She'll pitch a fit when she discovers those stitches though," Ben half-heartedly grinned deepening the lines etched around his eyes. "Girl always was particular about her hair. She's been out for hours, but that's good they said. Perhaps you should try some of that too, rest.."

"I will soon enough. I'd like to see her, if you don't mind." Quinn waited in the silence that lingered for Samantha's father to accept his request. A lot can be said in silence he was learning.

"I need to run over to the mill, let them know what's going on," Ben handed over the water pitcher to Quinn. "She'll be thirsty." Quinn accepted the chore gladly.

"Thank you, Henry. Thank you for finding her." Ben reached out, shook his hand, but Ben didn't release it. "I know you all found human remains up there. I didn't say anything to her, and she didn't seem to know about it."

"She didn't know because I covered her face. I couldn't let her see that." Quinn dropped his head. "I wish I didn't see it," Quinn added. Ben released his hand and placed it on Quinn's shoulder.

"Thank you for that too." Ben glanced about slowly. "I saw a news van out front and the nurses have orders not to let anyone on this end of the floor for now. I guess not everyone on that mountain knows how to hold their tongue. Either way, cats out of the bag. It's going to get a lot of attention."

"I should tell her before someone else does." Sam wasn't a fan of surprises, a fact that everyone knew.

"I should've done it already myself. She'd hate to know she stumbled over a body up there." Ben shook his head.

"There wasn't just one Ben. There are so many bones on that mountain, I don't know if they will ever know." Ben Carver's eyes went wide, but his lips remained firm.

"It could be an old Indian mound." Ben shifted uneasily, his voice low.

"The coroner says otherwise." Quinn sighed heavily. "It was like a mausoleum in there, and all I could think to do was cover her head and lie to her." Quinn chided himself.

"You found her, saved her, and protected my child." Ben squeezed his shoulder. "Sit out here for a bit, fetch some water and ice, and gather yourself up before you walk in there." Quinn lifted his chin. Man up, that's what Ben was telling him to do. Was that what he thought he was doing all those years after his wife died? Quinn of all people knew how to man up, but some things blew you over no matter how straight your spine was. "I'll be back in an hour or two. Don't reckon Nell's got room for me for a couple days?"

Quinn lifted a brow. "She always has room."

"I figure on staying close, helping where I can. If what you are saying is true, this is going to get a lot of attention. Sam doesn't even like singing with the choir. My girl likes keeping her head down," Ben smirked. It was a good thought, Ben being there and helping with the upcoming clients as well.

"I've got time owed to me too. Nelly said they have twelve coming this opening week alone. Not sure how many the second week, but Clark can't do that alone, and she needs to heal."

"Then it's settled," Ben nodded. A mutual agreement, a plan Sam wasn't aware of, was being made.

"She won't like it, but between the three of us, we can get through a couple weeks."

"Yes we can. I always liked you Henry, for a tree hugger that is," Ben smirked and aimed for the elevators. Denim from shoulder to ankle, a good three inches taller than Quinn, but his words left a hint of hope behind him.

Sam's mouth felt like cotton and her limbs wrung out like an old wash rag. The blanket felt warm, pleasantly heavy, and she slid down deeper to hold onto it a little longer. The scent of the mountain filled the room and if she wasn't mistaken, of a man. Sensing she wasn't alone in her room anymore, Sam opened her eyes.

"Afternoon sleepy head," Quinn said. He looked tired and like he had just wrested with a grizzly. His uniform was soiled and stained with barely any olive green showing.

And he was here. Why was he here?

"Where's Dad?" Her voice scratched.

"He had to go take care of things at work. He should be back in a bit. He's not left your side the whole time." Something in his tone was off. "Connie and Cindy and David have all been by too. The doctor said you're doing well. I think they're going to spring you tomorrow."

"I can't stay here that long. Brody?" Sam tried rising but she didn't have it in her to do the simple task. Quinn came to the bed-side and sat.

"Brody knows his momma fell on the hill and hurt her head and leg. When I left him he wanted to know if you would be wearing a cool cast he could sign," Sam smiled weakly. That sounded just like her son. Lifting her head tenderly with one strong arm, he tucked an extra pillow behind her. It was a common courtesy, so why did her breath seize just now?

"You checked in on my son?"

"It was on my list of things to do today," he said coolly giving her length a casual look over.

"Thank you," she managed and moved a finger to the side of her head. The tender sting, moist flesh she assumed was ointment, made her wince. She remembered now, in the sinkhole, he said Nelly took him for ice cream last night. Brody was probably eating up all the attention in her absence and if a stomachache was the result, Nelly would get an earful.

Quinn didn't move, instead he remained on the bed beside her. Those deep eyes looked at her as if he had never seen her a million times over the last twenty-years. "You're being nice. Why are you being nice? Do I have a brain tumor or something?" He didn't laugh. Didn't argue back either. Yeah, something was off with the forest ranger.

"I'm always nice. You just don't hear but what you want." His gaze continued roaming over her as if was picking out flaws and scars.

"I hear fine. One minute you're causing a scene at the Brick, the next you're pulling me out of a hole," Sam sighed. "You're a confusing man Henry Quinn."

"You caused a scene walking into the Brick in that short dress." His brows lifted in that same confident way that tempted her into an argument.

"My dress wasn't short. You were being ridiculous." She scoffed turning her focus to the wall. If she had two good legs and some clothes, she would walk out of the room. With two fingers he cautiously turned her to face him.

"You could see plumb to the thigh." His voice was calm but anger laced it.

"Legs. They're called legs. I nearly died and you're upset because God gave me legs? You've seen a hundred pair of them." She shrugged off a laugh and how warm his fingers felt on her skin.

"But those were your legs," he said pinning her with a look that held a certain possessiveness in it. "Nicer than a pair of twelve-year-old twigs but still very distracting." Perplexed, speechless, that's what she was and in light of her lack of witty comebacks Quinn inched closer. "Did I hear an apology somewhere in there?"

"Fine," she said sharply. "I guess I should apologize about Saturday. I don't normally bite and claw so easily and I didn't know Connie was taking me to the Brick." Her nose flared.

"I don't mind claws or teeth Sam," he grinned, "keeps things interesting." He toyed with her hair, letting the heavy locks drip between his fingers. "Let's just take breaks in between sparing. Be civil from time to time. And right now," he leaned back. "This is a good time." The sag in his shoulders told her just how much those words cost him.

A truce.

He was asking for a truce. Maybe finding her like he had shot some sense into him. Besides, harboring resentments was exhausting. She could handle a truce, for now.

"Did I do that?" She pointed to his face and winced.

"You are a hard rescue, but this one came from Roger Everett." So he got the local deer poacher, Sam thought with a grin. It was always nice to see that kind taken out of the mix of nature's natural cycle. She was happy for him, just as she always was when he made successful arrests. His work was dangerous too, that fact had not escaped her. How many times had she laid with an ear open, waiting for him to report in after some close calls. He was charmed, she had always thought.

"If you find a way to spring me today, I'll hold my tongue, not say a word to you for a month."

"I don't want you to hold your tongue. I prefer it when you are plenty capable of words, but I will see what I can do. If I can't spring you what will bringing Brody here get me?" He grinned again and this time Sam hated herself for how easily attracted she was.

"Same deal. Both get me what I want." She liked this Quinn, but it was best to remember under all those fine looks and that steady gaze, was a man who was untrustworthy. Hadn't Dale warned her about his ways? You couldn't be friends with some men without them getting the wrong impression, he said.

However, Quinn had thought of Brody. He came here to see her when his duty was over. He didn't have to. And he wanted a truce. Those were all important things. So why did that scare her?

"Samantha, why were you off the trail that far?"

"I do tend to do that Henry." She knew better than calling him that. *Too personal.* "I'm sorry I put you out." He said nothing, obviously taking this truce thing seriously. Sam let out a sigh and surrendered.

"I climbed into Clayton's old stand to look around, hydrate, and just listen to the quiet." It wasn't a lie.

"I didn't know you go up there," he said lowering his gaze. For all she had suffered in her losses, Quinn had always suffered more. She's do well to remember that.

"It's a rare thing, but I do." She swallowed. "I saw something. It was out of place, so I climbed down to see what it was. Sometimes balloons fall on the farm or some idiot riding across the trail to the park leaves their trash behind. It doesn't appeal to the eye." She toyed with her bed spread.

"You saw that bone," Quinn said and all his dark features tightened into a protective knot. "It was in your hand." She remembered but she was aware Quinn wanted something more from her. Did he want to know that on days when she felt lonely, she spoke to the mountain to fill her lonely void? That she missed having someone in her life?

"Then what?"

"It didn't look like a deer carcass and was too big for anything else I could think of, so I walked around, looking for more. That's when I heard a crack." She paused hearing the fracturing and splintering of wood as if it was happening again. "Then I realized I wasn't standing on dirt and leaves any more. I fell before I could react."

Silence floated between them. Quinn slowly got up from the bed.

"I lied to you," he admitted.

"Lied?" She tilted her head for a better look at him. "I don't understand, and you're being way too serious right now."

"When I covered your face and told you it was to protect you from debris. I lied." He stared out the large two-story window, a man pondering the world, or shouldering it. She wasn't sure which.

"And the purpose of that was?"

"Before they lowered the basket to get you out, you kept falling in and out of consciousness. I saw something on one of the walls and shined the light on it." His body became rigid, obviously disturbed. Staring out the window, collecting his thoughts, Quinn stood silent.

"What did you see Quinn?" She prodded. Why was he speaking in riddles?

"Bones," he said bluntly, his focus still landing on the cold grim world outside. Sam gasped.

"You mean there was a dead animal down there with me?" That made her skin crawl. Had it been a bear?

"It wasn't an animal Sam." He turned, faced her with a ghostly expression.

"A person!" The words burst out of her before she could rein them back. "Are you telling me I fell in a hole with a dead body?" Goosebumps rode wildly over her body. Her first thought, as she assumed anyone who lived in Milford first thought would be, was it was her. It was her best friend. All these years, she had never been found and now... Sam tried to keep her breathing level as she went back to that November night and replayed the details in her head.

Becky hadn't fallen in that hole too. She was taken. Sam had seen her in the truck, heard her scream for Jake to save her. A person didn't forget such details as the ones she had forever burned in her memory.

""Henry, was it..." she bit her lip on saying the name. She couldn't bear saying her name.

"No," he shook his head and moved back to her clearly seeing how she could have thought it was possible.

"It was something else." Taking her hand, Quinn painfully described what he discovered over the next few minutes. In all her years working dispatch, nothing like this had ever come over the wire. Sam had thought herself immune to shock and awe. Disturbing matters rolled off the cuff. They had to get the job done. Looking up, the man of steely resolve and dark gazes sat focused on their hands intertwined, she recognized how weak they both were.

He had been rocked by what he had seen. Watching him, listening to the eerie details of secret earthy room of bones and bugs disturbed her more than knowing she had lain in the scatter of them.

"There were so many of them," his voice drew to a whisper. The way he held her fingers, focusing on each slender digit, told what he witnessed taunted him now. He was beside himself and she had never seen him unsteady before. Instinct swallowed all reason and she placed her free hand over his, sandwiching him in comfort.

"Bones, you saw lots of bones," she said trying to absorb the reality of his words.

"Bodies," he corrected. "It wasn't just scattered bones Sam. It was the remains of multiple bodies." If she thought nothing could further shock her, she had just proved that wrong.

"You're saying there are a bunch of bodies in a hole on our mountain? That I fell… I touched…" she couldn't breathe. Was she having a panic attack?

"Calm down Sam. Breathe for me." She couldn't, even if she wanted to. The mental image in her head wouldn't allow for it. She had thought she was dreaming, or dying. That in her moments of fading in and out of consciousness, she believed she had seen death, his thin legs and smiling eyes.

"I said breathe Samantha." He ordered sharply, snapping her back to present. "Breathe or I'll get the whole staff in here to make you." His threat willed her temper to take over and with that came air. She focused on his eyes, sharp as the Cooper's Hawk spotting his prey. Sweet air dove into her lungs. With both hands on her shoulders, he gave her a shake as if that helped anything.

"Stop yelling at me," the words vibrated out of her as she slapped at him in protest. Surely finding out you spent over nine hours in a mass grave earned a not-so-subtle reaction.

"You're gonna be the death of me woman," his shoulders rose and sunk as if hiking Everest.

"I'm fine. Don't touch me." She barked. Ignoring her command, Quinn went to the bathroom and returned with a damp cloth.

"Don't do that again. You scared me plenty last night." He pressed the rag to her face and dared her to kick up a fuss.

"You're not the one who fell in a hole with a bunch of dead people." The water felt cool on her hot skin.

"No, I just had to find you lying with them," he countered. Suddenly his pale expressions and uneasiness made sense. She had scared him.

"There is going to be a lot going on the next few days. Press is already parked outside the hospital. Ben is staying at the house and the sheriff has posted no trespassing signs along the drive." Quinn continued as she worked to get her breath to flow more evenly.

"I don't expect them to follow the rules. No more than last time." Sam closed her eyes, letting it all sink in. She hadn't remembered being this tired before, but she needed to know what else to expect.

"I'm sorry I had to be the one to tell you. I'm sorry it's moving so fast, that can't be helped. I'm sorry it was you that found them. I'm sorry it was there of all places." He blew out a breath.

"I'm sorry about all of those things too."

"The sheriff will need to talk to you, but he said he would give you time to get home first." There was more he wasn't telling her, but Sam wasn't about to prod further right now.

One problem at a time. It was her life's motto.

"I'll go see about getting you out of here." He slowly let go of her hand and got to his feet again. She missed his nearness immediately. As he strolled to the door, she called out to him.

"Henry." he turned slowly. "I'm sorry." He nodded and was gone.

CHAPTER EIGHT

Not wanting to be a further burden than she felt she was, Sam carefully slid out of the truck seat before Quinn reached her. Ashen clouds moved steadily across a purple evening sky.

"Home," her heart whispered.

"Let me help you up those steps," Quinn insisted, taking her free arm.

"I've got it," she replied quickly, crutching her way to the porch.

"Still stubborn I see." He remarked opening the front door, letting her wobble inside. They hadn't said a word on the drive home, each having plenty to occupy their thoughts. She was grateful for all he had done, but seeing Brody was of utmost importance right now.

"You've done plenty. I'm grateful," Sam said in an honest tone. "But I can take care of myself." She only faced him to prove herself capable of not crumpling her placid facade under his dark gaze and strong build. Too much of Henry Quinn was weakening her independence. In fact, if he swept her up in those strong arms and carried her up those stairs, she would have protested, but not complained. She blinked away the thought before he read her mind and her defenses were blown.

"I never doubted it, but..." The sound of running feet prevented his next words, thankfully.

Brody rushed into the foyer to greet her, but slid to a halt a good five feet away. Blue eyes, her eyes, widened as he took in the look of her before his gaze traveled to Quinn sporting his own bruises.

His little knees were dirty. Playing with his trucks in the hallway again she figured. His dark brown shirt was lopsided where he had buttoned it himself. Slowly the sole recipient of all her love inched closer. Her arms ached to hold him. "I'm good bub. I'm just a little sore."

"Can I.." He bit his lip exposing a gap between his teeth. Feet sliding, he inched closer. She admired his control, a rare thing for someone so young. She liked to think he got that from her. Dale had never been patient.

She adjusted her crutch, just precaution while her knee healed from the tears and pulled ligaments, and put out an arm. "Come here sweetie. A hug will make it all better." Her signature words for healing hurts. Two little arms locked around her middle and everything else vanished in an instant.

Sam buried her face into his unruly brown hair. He smelled of sugar cookies and little boy and she breathed it in like a starved animal. This was her reason for living, her reason for being, and she thanked God silently as Brody's arms tightened for not taking another parent away from him.

"They said you fell in a hole and now there's all kinds of people who want to take your picture." Sam cringed. Nine stitches lay carefully hidden under her hair. A bare spot needed to close the fleshy gap, but its placement on the back of her head was easily concealed and she most certainly didn't want her picture taken.

"You know your mom doesn't like her picture taken," Quinn put in as if knowing anything about what she liked and didn't. Brody stepped out of her hold and searched her for more injuries, stopping his gaze on the blue brace wrapped around her left knee. The sweats Nelly packed her were loose and rarely worn, but a whole lot easier to climb into, but it was a shame to cut such comfy clothes. Those took years to fit right.

"This is just until my knee gets stronger. A couple of days and I'll be fit as a fiddle. I can't lift you, yet, but I can hug and tickle just fine." She showed him, sending him into immediate giggles. Nelly came into the hallway, a red dishtowel slung over one shoulder.

"Well, let's get your momma up to bed. She needs to rest and you can help Nana with supper tonight." Nelly clamped on to both his shoulders. "He has turned out to be a better dish washer than you anyhow." Nelly grinned. The woman was a saint. Here she had lost so much and managed to smile and mother every soul that came within a mile of her.

"I'm not tired Nelly, and I still need to go over plans with Clark. I texted him on the way over, so I should probably set an extra plate for dinner." Sam crutched forward, following Nelly towards the kitchen.

"You can rest until he gets here." Quinn said, setting her hospital bag and medicine on the kitchen table. "Brody, can you be responsible and help your mom to her room?" Brody perked, and scooped up her good hand.

"Yes, I can do it. Come on Mom," Brody said, puffing out his chest. Quinn ruffled his hair playfully before Brody lured her away. A nasty trick, Sam thought, using her son against her. Sam shot a frozen glare over her shoulder to Quinn before navigating the stairs on one good leg.

"Thank you for the ride home, but I've got this now," Sam clipped out, hoping he wasn't still there when she came back down for supper

Quinn did go, but only long enough to gather a few things. He showered, packed, called in to his supervisor and explained the situation best he could. He tried not to think what was happening on the mountain currently, the excavating, cataloging, and identifying of all those lost souls. Quinn's focus was here, on the souls living behind these walls. Everyone he truly cared about.

Using vacation time due him, he was free to help Clark with the incoming hunters, and hopefully they had plenty of spots on this side of the mountain to steer clear of all the happenings.

Ben's old beater Ford and Clark's new Chevy sat outside. He also expected Connie and Matt to drop by if they hadn't already. He could smell meatloaf. Nelly never disappointed when it came to cooking.

Bones on the Mountain

He stood on this side of the deer engraved door. Why was he hesitating going inside his aunt's house? It felt silly to knock on the door that he once called home, but he did it anyway.

The door swung open revealing his younger cousin. "Why are you knocking? This is sort of your house too." Clark questioned taking a step back so Quinn could enter. His eyes immediately caught sight of the duffle bag in Quinn's hand. "Never mind," Clark smiled. Of course that didn't make Quinn feel any more confident about his newest decision.

"I'm taking over her part of it. She just doesn't know it yet." Quinn said casually.

"That's good to hear. Between you and Ben we will have it covered. But I have a feeling not everyone is going to like it. She's stubborn and a bit…controlling."

"She's not the only one," Quinn said firmly.

"This is going to make for a very interesting two weeks, and I got front row seats. They're all in the kitchen. Nell's finishing up supper." Clark chuckled and started down the hall littered with toy trucks and soldiers. Quinn shucked off his boots and followed.

Stepping into the kitchen, an immediate sense of home washed over him. His small two bedroom house in the next town served a purpose, but even after all these years it never felt like a home, just a place to put your things and lay your head.

"Quinn!" Brody ran in, a pair of new pricey red wing boots, one over his pant leg, one under it, clamping against the hardwood floor before he bounced into Quinn's arms. He was growing like a weed. Quinn tousled his hair again and sat him back down. "Sit with me," Brody said excited and pulled him towards the table. "Nana made meatloaf."

"So I smelled," Quinn responded. "Nice boots." Brody lifted a foot, flashed it proudly as Sam limped into the room. She was freshly showered, the ends of her hair still damp, and changed into a pair of loose-fitting jeans and pullover jersey sweater. She'd already shed the brace from the hospital, but Quinn noted the swelling at the knee and was glad she at least had the good sense to keep it wrapped. The crutch tucked roughly under her arm helped as she aimed to assist Nelly. That was Sam, always pushing on, dealing with whatever life threw at her. And life had thrown a lot her way.

When her head lifted and those deep blue eyes caught his, she bristled. It wasn't the reaction Quinn hoped for. He sat in his normal seat, leaned back in his chair, and studied her carefully in case she needed help.

"Boy's got finer footwear then I do," Ben jested still wearing nothing but denim. In fact, now that Quinn thought about it, he had never seen Ben Carver in anything else.

"You and me both," Quinn added. Sam gathered utensils next, crutched them over, and then returned for a pitcher of tea. Why no one was addressing that she should take it easy, he hadn't a clue. He thought to help her, scooted his seat back just a hair, testing, but got...the look. All men knew that one. Her eyes were arresting, storm surge blue under thick lashes, and her lips pressed firmly together. She was going to crack a tooth doing that.

"Hand that over before you fall on your face dork," Clark jested. They were close, like siblings bonded without blood. Clark could tease, poke, and praise, and Sam always forgave him. Quinn never got any such mercies. He left her for college and she hadn't forgotten

The tension in the air was thick, but no one wanted to discuss what was taking place on the mountain right now, the safe removal of the remains, in front of a seven-year-old. Quinn had conjured up a few scenarios on his drive over, but none held much worth as to how so many died in one place without anyone being the wiser.

The meal consisted of hearty food, and everyone being entertained by Brody It was a brief reprieve from the last 24 hours and Quinn welcomed it as much as the rest of them. After the meal, Quinn shook hands with Ben, as he was due to head out for his last shift. Ben high fived Brody, thanked Nelly for a good meal, and walked with Sam to the front door.

Quinn stood and started clearing the table, but watched as father and daughter whispered back and forth. Ben touched her cheek, the scratches pink on her jaw, with fatherly affection and Sam hugged him before he left.

"I'll help Nelly with clean- up. You can say good night to Brody before you leave," Sam said entering the kitchen.

"I'm not leaving." He followed her to the sink carrying a few glasses. "I'm staying." Pretending to ignore him, she began running the dish water. She wasn't going to make this easy for either of them.

"Nelly enjoys your visits, but it's been a long day for all of us."

"You need help. Might be a little tricky on crutches, and how do you plan on driving men out there, sitting in the cold all day, getting into the stand with your camera gear?" She flinched, obviously not having thought it out thoroughly.

"Clark will help. You have your own job, maybe you should go do that." She floated him a challenging look.

"I asked him to come," Clark announced, but she wasn't fooled and ignored him.

"I haven't taken off work in ten years. I'm due some time." If she thought that look would persuade him, she was mistaken. "I'm staying." Quinn watched her work hard for a reply. This was as much his home as it was hers.

"We run a business here. You won't be bringing your...*toys* around my son. I'm trying to raise a good man and he doesn't need to be exposed to the perks of bachelorhood."

Quinn lifted a brow. What was she thinking? In fact when was the last time he even dated?

"I grew out of needing toys a long time ago," he said angrily scrapping mashed potatoes into a plastic container. He dropped the large spoon into the dishwater with a splash. That ought to cool her down.

"Nell, you save corn too?" Quinn turned and asked as Sam grumbled beside him toweling off her sweatshirt. He noted the wide grin spread on Nelly's face as she spooned another helping of ice cream on Brody and Clark's cobbler.

"Makes the best corn cakes," Nelly said in sing-song fashion and a laugh in her voice. Glad someone was enjoying herself. He turned, covered the plastic container and dunked the empty glass bowl in the dishwater. Taking up the dish cloth, he gave it a good cleaning and placed it in the rack. Standing this close he had to address it. They would be living under the same roof for the next couple of weeks.

"Your opinion of me…hurts a little," he continued.

"Call them like I see them. A skunk doesn't change its smell," she elbowed him out of her way as she dunked the drinking glasses next. Seeing everyone focused on Brody, Quinn stepped behind her, leaning in until she was pressed into the sink, and whispered. "Neither do you. Jasmine. You still smell like Jasmine." He heard her breath catch, felt her body tense, and tried not to grin. Satisfied he closed down her next insult, Quinn stepped away.

Scooping up Brody, Quinn gave him a tickle and wrestled him over his shoulder. "I think this one could use a bath," he sniffed his hostage, "because he stinks." Brody giggled and wiggled in protest. He was going to be tall, legs as willowy as his mother's.

"You stink more," Brody cackled.

"It's good to have family. Don't you think Sam?" Nelly quickly added. Her eyes beamed at the thought. "It's a blessing." Sam's shoulders lowered at Nelly's question. She glanced at him, Brody wiggling like a can of worms on his shoulder. No one would disagree that family was everything.

"I'll go show Henry where he can sleep and lay out Brody's nightclothes. You and Clark take care of your plans." Sam's lips remained closed and she nodded a thank you to her elder.

"Samantha," Quinn stopped and turned. She was trying on a fit of angry, but this time Quinn saw right through it. "You *have* raised a pretty great kid." He didn't wait for her response and swept Brody over his shoulder again, carting him up the stairs in flying superman formation.

"You knew he was staying didn't you," she snapped at Clark.

"Found out five minutes before you. Face it Sam, he can do it and you need to let that leg heal. We're lucky to have him." Lucky or not the very thought of Henry Quinn sleeping under the same roof as her sent a fresh panic through her. They were professionals, she reminded herself once more. *Focus on that.* She would just ignore him. How hard could it be?

"Dad's helping too." She was pleased to have her father around. Brody rarely had time with him. As she and Clark worked out new plans, she hoped two of the clients who thought they would be put in line with a good chance at Zeus wouldn't be disappointed. No one had to tell her the northwestern side of the mountain was now off limits. She knew.

"I think we can sit two of those Pollard brothers on this rise, here and here," Clark pointed at their napkin drawing of the farm. It was always best to work out details before guests arrived. Sam liked following a plan as did Clark, which was why they worked so well together.

"I think that's best. What about the cameras. We promise on our site we will record their experience as part of the package. I can't imagine your Neanderthal cousin knowing the lens from the flash."

"Don't worry Sam. We have this all under control." Clark said touching her hand in assurance. That's what she was afraid of.

CHAPTER NINE

On the second floor Quinn wiggled Brody off his shoulder. Pine adorned walls and log railing had replaced old Victorian wallpaper and carpet floors. It competed well alongside larger hunting outfits, but Quinn longed in a thread of nostalgia, missing the halls of his childhood.

"Brody, run and get your bath things while I show Henry his room," Aunt Nelly instructed.

"He can sleep in my room," Brody said eagerly, stirring a laugh.

"Might try that out another night, bub. Go on now, get your things as Nana asked." Quinn grinned and watched him run inside. He had always wanted children, a few really. Dale honoring him as Brody's guardian had been a blessing. For that, Quinn was thankful.

"He looks up to you," Nelly turned to face him.

"He doesn't know any better," Quinn smirked. "Now, where do you want me?" he asked. Nelly pivoted and walked to the right of the wooden staircase.

"This should work for now. I have the other rooms ready for guests and don't want you messing them up." She forgot he was no longer ten apparently. Since his boyhood days Quinn had acquired a taste for order. Made things easier to find.

Quinn stood with both arms down his sides in the doorway. "This is...her room," Quinn said, his stomach no longer content with a full meal, but rather souring as he stood outside the room Sam and Dale shared.

"It was Dale's," Nelly said firmly, crossing her arms as if chilled. "Sam hasn't slept in here for over ten years." That quick nonchalant answer only puzzled him more.

"We women know everything." Nelly said flatly, reading his thoughts. She had always been good at that. "You think I didn't know my own children?" She quipped.

"But... she stayed?" Quinn couldn't understand it. If Sam knew her husband had done more than occasionally dance with a woman, why didn't she pack up Brody and leave?

"His sins weren't hers to carry, but she stayed for Brody. And part of me likes to think, she stayed for me too. She doesn't say it, but she loves me. Poor thing tolerates me stepping on her toes every day. She could have taken that insurance money and started a new life anywhere. I told her as much too, but this is her home." Quinn felt his heart tighten. "The only real home she has ever had." Quinn hadn't looked at it from that view and now that he was, he was appreciated his aunt all the more.

"And since I know my children well, I have something to say to you."

"Alright," he straightened his shoulders.

"We taught you to be a good man. Honorable and good-hearted." Quinn nodded. "You are all of those things so don't disappoint me."

"What do you mean?" Nelly pointed a boney finger, her hazel eyes flicked with green.

"Don't you go awakening a heart you don't intend to love," Nelly ordered. "That's the cruelest thing a man can do." Surprise caught him unguarded for a second, then with a wide smile Quinn pulled Nelly into a hug, her small frame literally disappearing under him. Nelly Quinn was quite a woman indeed. She was a nurturer, leader, and all out mind reader.

"I have no intentions to start anything I can't see through to the end," he said and kissed her cheek.

Sam climbed the stairs after Clark left. She needed to tuck Brody in, and slip into her own bed for a while. The headache wasn't letting up. She had swallowed the large pill prescribed, but regretted needing it. She never liked taking medicine, even a Tylenol if she could help it.

Quinn would be sleeping under the same roof. She couldn't get the troublesome thought out of her head. More troubling was that Quinn walked into her world and was taking it over. He had always been the largest man in the room even when he wasn't.

She wanted to refuse his help, but Nelly had come downstairs, humming. Brody was sparkling the same way he did when she told him they were going to the zoo. Sam had heard them earlier running around like the house was on fire. Everyone was over the moon that Henry Quinn was home, but her.

Despite all the good he did, she couldn't see past the real Quinn. He led Dale astray, but then again, Dale had chosen to follow. They were two peas of the same pod, charming and handsome, and scoundrels.

At the top of the landing, Sam stilled noting the shadow down the hall. She figured Nelly would put him in the big room at the end of the hall, only the best for Quinn, she silently vexed.

Why did he have to look so good? That long tall athlete she met on the ball field had aged well. She had secretly crushed over Henry for weeks after that first encounter. But he was a senior, and she not yet even in high school. She figured most girls crushed that way.

When Becky welcomed her to Milford and became her new best friend, Sam had to admit she spent more nights at the Quinn house than her own hoping to sneak a peek at the college jock. Instead of girly make overs or learning Nelly's cookie recipes, it was him she was eager to talk with. He had been a great listener then.

As she grew into her legs and grew out of those ridiculous training bras, Sam barely had a glance at the heartthrob that once kept her awake at night. Henry Quinn was off living life with friends and girls who looked a whole lot prettier than her. She finally faced the fact no man would look at her like she hoped and couldn't believe there was a time she wanted to be one of those women with the painted face and the tight skirts.

Sam grew up and found jeans and boots and braids suited her style just fine. Then Dale's presence went from Becky's annoying flirty brother to her first and only boyfriend. If she hadn't taken Jenny Schroon's dare, she would have never gone out with him on that first date. She hadn't anticipated Felicity Brown in the equation, or that Dale actually liked her more than the stunning red head all the boys chased after. He never acted serious about any girl in school. And they had something important in common.

Becky.

After Becky vanished, Dale was there. He held her, cried with her, and made her feel less than the failure her thirteen-year-old self felt. Sam thought if she had only tried harder with the dispatcher, sounded more serious and not a hysterical child, maybe the woman wouldn't have thought the call a prank. Maybe she could have gotten help faster. Becky could have grown up, married, and had children of her own. The thought brought on a few tears as it always did. Who knew why God put one person in your life and took another like He did.

Quinn turned and found her watching him. His essence had already penetrated the air. Like the girl on the ball field, her stomach fluttered. She would never again let a Quinn get under her skin.

"You didn't share this room together." It wasn't a question he was asking, it was an acknowledgment. Her heart stopped. Quinn couldn't have stabbed her harder if he had a knife. No one woman wants to look back on such reminders of their weakness. It was none of Quinn's business if her son wore expensive boots, or if she slept in the same bed as her husband. He needed to mind his own business..

"No."

"I'm sorry," he managed to say. "You deserved better." She thought she did too. Still, having those words come from him didn't clean the slate.

"You hung out with him practically every night. You knew him way better than me, so what did you expect?" She pushed despite telling herself she would never pursue answers to questions she didn't really want to know. She watched his brows gather, confusion wearing heavy on his strong features.

"I loved him. We were family. But Sam, I have never once hung out with him and we barely spoke since the day he married you." Sam gasped at his bold-faced lie. All those meet-ups and overnights, Henry had missed the wedding, and Clark had to literally force him to come meet Brody that first time.

"Good night Samantha." He turned and slipped into guest room three. All plain and pine and like the elk head Sam knew hung over the old iron bed he would be sleeping under, she had misjudged her strength. Henry Quinn could still crush her with barely a word.

Bones on the Mountain

Across the river, he tossed and turned on the polyester cot. Sleep wasn't coming tonight between wearing all these layers, working such long hours, and hands that ached from too many turns of a wrench. He prided himself on being stronger than people thought. He was stronger than they thought.

He rolled on his left side and still found no comfort there. He'd much rather be home, in his own bed. A man didn't scoff such privileges as that. There were years he'd been lucky to get a cold floor for sleeping, but that was before he learned a man could change his fate. All he had to do was eliminate any obstacles in his way. Like his mother's cat, he thought with a grin. That menacing worthless creature ate better than he did, until he didn't.

Locking his fingers behind his head, he smiled at the memory. They didn't think he would do it, and yet, he did. They didn't think he would do much of anything now did they. Satisfied with knowing he proved them wrong, he pondered over his next plunder.

His recent visit up the mountain had helped a little. A year was a long time to wait for a man to feed his soul. Closing his eyes he saw them. Each prize he won for being the best at what he did. Now he just had to decide. Would he take another stray, or this year, would he capture the ultimate prize?

He made a mental list of what he would need. He never wrote it down. Only idiots made list. He should probably see to working on the truck on his next days off. You always made sure everything was in running order just in case.

He would need a better tactic too. When he was younger, a few cheap lines was enough, but last year had been a close one.

Sweet Kelsey, he thought with a smile. She was on to him too quick. Perhaps his looks were slipping. He never did like teachers, but he did like Kelsey. Perhaps heading north, taking one last look before deciding what this year would bring him was best.

Finally tired, he rolled to his right and the cold concrete wall. He'd put away his *list* for now, Oh, he almost forgot he needed to pick up so more kibble soon. His friends were likely missing him.

CHAPTER TEN

Ron Culver pulled up to the Deer Creek Lodge with a gut full of gravel. There were times in a man's life when he had to do things he didn't want to, and this was that time. He exited the patrol car, covered his bald head with his sheriff's cap and rolled his shoulders. He fitted the button through the buttonhole of his shirt at the belly where things got a little tighter. He preferred stirring a laugh, never did like tears, but there would be no way around those today. Before this professional visit was over, tears would be all he would leave behind. He only hoped Nelly could forgive the messenger. He had already broken her heart plenty as it was.

The two-story lodge had transformed from the nice big farm house he remembered. It had been white with black shutters and a stone foundation when Clayton's folks inherited it. Now wood stained logs lifted its stature into a worthy retreat. A lot of money had been paid to spiff it up to this caliber. Two widowed women managed to turn a little hunting business into something that brought revenue into this small nowhere town. He liked seeing his town grow and prosper, and noted that in the last few years, the Deer Creek Lodge was encouraging other business's to ramp up their styles. Newer paint, cozy porches, and homemade goods were drawing in weekenders who wanted a taste of the simple life. Milford even had an archery range and outdoor supply store opening this past year alone.

Milford also had death. Too much of it for his liking.

Reaching the front porch, Quinn stepped out without the uniform he usually donned and looking more at home than Ron had seen him in years. It was good that he was here. It made Ron's job easier. The fella had handled everything well enough so far and he wasn't no stranger to handling what he had to.

"Have they finished up there?" Quinn asked sipping a steamy cup.

"Not yet. Never seen so many people dressed like aliens." Quinn quirked a brow. "FBI sent in a team to do the hard part. They have multiple agencies working the angles, pulling out old cold cases, and hoping to give them all identities." Ron removed his hat, shook his head. "If they can," he said skeptical. "With so many, and from what they know so far, the victims weren't all killed at the same time." Quinn's brows gathered but he didn't say a word. He was a smart one, but Ron knew even he couldn't have predicted the recent discovery.

"Ben was waging on it being just an Indian mound." Quinn leaned on a porch post, crossing his legs at the ankle. Ron could see he was already gathering assumptions. This was not going to be easy.

"That I could have wrapped my head around, or even a bunch of hippies who decided to drink the Kool Aid," Ron shook his head. "They're all female. Ages haven't been determined yet, but they're certain they have a killer on their hands." Ron removed his hat and rubbed his head. He could still picture the scene in his head. What kind of monster not only killed but was disturbed enough to display some of his victims like that. Several skeletons were fully intact and embedded into the rich clay mud, while others scattered the corners in crates to be forgotten. *And the beetles.* Apparently the FBI thought a bunch of bugs meant something. Of course forensics sometimes used insects to help determine time of death, but there was nothing but bones left. It was a mystery his small-town knowledge lacked knowing.

"Think he's local?" Quinn looked out towards the mountain. It hadn't escaped Ron that any monster who could kill without regard to human life, showcase them like portraits, could be someone they knew.

"I hope not. Can't imagine anyone from here like that. They've been bagging up those bugs all morning too."

"The beetles?"

"Yeah. Debriefing is in a couple hours, thought you might want to join me and David in that."

"Not sure I want to be more a part of it than I was," Quinn said directly without sway in his tone.

"Agent Dorsey, he's the one in charge." Ron stepped closer. "Well Quinn, he requested you." Ron watched his face shift. " You're part of it like it or not."

"Well this can't get any worse," Quinn grumbled. It was clear the last thing he wanted was to be more mixed up in the case than merely discovering it. Ron dug deep in his gut. He didn't like this part of the job.

"It gets a whole lot worse," Ron informed him cautiously.

"Samantha fell into a mass grave of possible murdered women and almost lost her life. I had to see her, in there, like that. We could have lost her up there," Quinn's pointed. "This house has endured enough. I'm off for a few weeks to help with the upcoming hunt. I need to be here."

The sheriff pinned him with a look. His thick bushy brows gathered painfully and if he twisted that hat in his hand any more, he might be needing another one.

Murdered women, Quinn rewound his own words. In Ron's silence Quinn felt his heart begin to race even before his mind could decipher why.

"I'm sorry Quinn," Ron offered before placing a hand of confirmation on his shoulder. "The first two sets of remains have been identified." Fact and coincidence crashed like a waves on rock. Quinn's knees weakened as everything he feared, was confirmed.

"No." Quinn breathed out. Ron's crestfallen look awoke Quinn's worst nightmares. He had a million of them over the years since Becky disappeared. "You mean. Oh God. Hold on," He bent forward when his knees jellied in the reality of what the sheriff was trying not to say. His cup crashed onto the porch, spilling it contents. His breakfast of fried eggs, toast, and bacon climbed up his throat, singed the lining while his stomach wretched a horrible jolt. This could not be happening, he told himself as he fought for air. The hand on his shoulder tightened.

"You take a minute. Take twenty if you need them. I'm here with you until you're ready."

Ready to stand, ready to breathe, or ready to accept? Quinn would never be ready for any of those things. Not now.

"She's been here...this close...all this time?" He had shed enough tears when he was young for the little girl he loved like a sister. Figured he had dried them up for a lifetime by now. That's when he learned to accept that some things a man may never know. He covered his face with his palm. Not for hiding sensitivities, but closing off reality as it clawed into his heart.

"I plan to go chat with Jake Foster later," Ron added. Quinn sucked in the cold air, let it burn so he could feel something less painful than what his heart was doing. Even mentioning Jake's name brought on a fresh wave of painful memories.

"Jake doesn't know where his dad is, Ron. I still believe he never did. He's a lot of things, but a liar was never one of them. That man took her and put Becky up there to laugh at us, mocking us all these years?"

Many felt Jake's dad, Larry Foster, had been responsible for Becky's disappearance. The license plate and vehicle description Sam reported matched and linked the two. And though she hadn't seen the driver's face, Jake hadn't recognized him and he had a closer look, chasing after the truck as he had. The sheriff believed Jake was only covering for his dad, some thought he even had a hand in it, but Quinn didn't believe any of that. Jake hated his abusive father and would have used the incident to get him free of the wrath of him. And Jake was broken. From that night on the scared boy he once knew became something else altogether.

The kink in the whole investigation was that Larry Foster was accounted for that night, he hadn't clocked into work at the local electric company the next day. No one had seen or heard from him since. Another cold case that would never be solved, the FBI told Nelly and Clayton two years after that fateful night. Quinn learned early in life that sometimes, bad guys did win and little girls simply vanished without a trace.

"Do you know for sure that it's her?"

"Dental records confirmed it. They're still working on others. Casey McCloud is helping the state medical examiner and the FBI is sending them more help. I let them have the old newspaper office to use. We'll both know a lot more this evening."

The sound of Aunt Nelly and Sam drifted out. Both men started at the door. They both knew what came next.

"I'm truly sorry Quinn," Ron shuffled. Quinn got to his feet and supported himself on the porch railing. He couldn't let Nelly see him like this.

"I've re-opened the case. I promised long ago I'd find her, and as much as it pains me to do this to her, again," Ron paused, placed his hat back on his head. "I reckon its time she knows her Becky has finally been found."

Quinn watched his elder's shoulder straighten, but his eyes, they didn't hide how hard this was for him too. Ron had made Nelly a promise but now he had a second chance to find the man who took one of their own out of her back yard.

Ron was surprised how well Nelly and Sam took the news. He expected tears, got them too, but when Nelly poured him a cup of coffee, offered him a slice of chocolate cake, he found her strength still as impressive as the grieving mother all those years ago. All mothers hope for the best, pray to hold their lost children again, but after five years of searching, Nelly had accepted she might never see Becky again.

Closure for her was putting her child to rest with her family. She asked only one thing of him. *One.* Find the man who took babies from their families. And of course, Ron promised he would. Now it was time to make good on that.

Thirty-four-year-old Jake Foster was the town's only mechanic. His smart mouth matched with those rugged good looks got him in as much trouble as it got him feminine attention. Ron remembered the talented boy that was raised hard. The young man who helped the high school football team win the state championship three years in a row, and the same one who was a suspect in a missing person's case.

He parked his patrol car under the Jake's Garage sign next to two nice rigs worth more than his annual salary. Now that he delivered the news to the Quinn's, the real work needed to be started. The bones on the mountain indicated a serial killer had entered their small town at some point and finding the Quinn girl meant it was time to re-question the boy who was seen with her last. All the evidence pointed to Larry Foster. Was it possible he was under their nose all this time just as Becky Quinn had been, hiding somewhere in the mountain range spanning multiple counties? Ron had heard of men capable of living off grid, out of sight. They even started making TV shows about that stuff. If Larry Foster was still nearby, Jake would know.

The sound of rock music bounced off the service bay walls of the garage. Jake was a master mechanic, could fix and drive anything with wheels, but he never outgrew his wild youth . Ron stepped inside, spotted the old radio on a ply-board platform next to the door, and clicked it off. An oil-stained set of jeans sticking out of a fairly new Dodge Charger moved, then the rest of the body rolled out from under the car, presenting the man in whole.

"Got something against Def Leopard?" Jake gave him a scowl and slowly got to his feet. The shaggy haired boy he once pitied when he became sheriff looked about the same given a few more pounds, as he did nineteen years ago. Only now Ron Culver held everything but pity for the menace. Jake had been busted three times for marijuana and drunk in public, and four times for fighting . Some kids simply could not outgrow the parents they were born to no matter how many local giving hearts dropped their charities onto them.

"Need to talk." Ron leaned against a cluttered work station. Wiping his hands on a shop rag, Jake sauntered over to a fridge, pulled out two beers and offered Ron one. "You know I don't drink, Jake." Jake smiled popping the top and took a hard swig.

"You should start. Then you wouldn't look so serious and mad all the time." Jake said. "And if this is about the man who got my mother knocked up, I don't know any more today than I did then." He took another swig, tossed the bottle in a nearby can, and opened the other. "Rumors spread fast around here, and I saw the news van roll into town yesterday. They so much as step in this garage I'll send them packing. I'm not living through all of that a second time."

"No getting around it," Ron said bluntly. "You have to know something. You and Sam were the last ones to see her. It's time you stop protecting your daddy and talk to me."

Jake laughed and Ron felt his fuse shorten. "Well I only heard they might have found her, thanks for the gentle confirmation sheriff." Jake gritted his teeth together. "And I would hand him to you on a silver platter, but truth is Sheriff, I don't know where he is and I still don't believe it was him in the truck. I may have been a scared boy back then, but I know what I saw. You can cross your arms and shoot me glares all day long, but I cared for her. The man behind that wheel wasn't my dad. He was half dad's age, blonde too. He had a beard and a hat. I told you all of this years ago."

"I will find him, and if you're lying, I'll know," Ron pushed off the bench and strolled to the open air.

"Sheriff," Ron turned. "Are they positive?" For a second Ron could see the distraught heartbroken kid again. Maybe Quinn was right. Even if Jake thought it was someone else, he wasn't lying. He believed what he saw.

"I can't say officially, but you might want to see Nelly in a day or two once she's had a moment to gather herself." That was the best he could do, under the law. And for the first time in Jake Foster's life he thanked him, then strolled back inside and flipped on his radio.

CHAPTER ELEVEN

If they can't look you in the eye,
they're either hiding a secret or a love.

Quinn stepped into the old newspaper office wandering what the heck he was doing here. The last place he wanted to be was where Sheriff Culver called Ground Zero. Ceiling to wall windows were blocked by dark drapes and cardboard. Walls of grey surrounded the room with faded brown tile floors beneath. He watched Casey McCloud, the local coroner, and two men in white coats carefully puzzle together a skeleton. He bristled, trying not to let the fact that Becky was possibly here bother him. There were more than twenty foldout tables and others attempting the same process in the open space while three dark suits conversed at a paper laden desk in the corner. Phones rang, some buzzed, but everything and everyone was moving, doing their job to help identify and ease grieving families who had lost loved ones.

Casey turned and caught him standing in the doorway. She was Nelly's age. Short brown hair with strings of silver freely woven in. Smart enough to accept her age or smart enough not to let the town's only hair stylist have a whack at her. Quinn stood rigid when she strolled over.

"I'm sorry Quinn," Casey offered a hug. "Did you come to see her?"

"My presence was requested or I wouldn't be here." Casey nodded her head in understanding. Quinn would rather remember the young Becky, beautiful and vibrant with life, than what one of these tables held of her remains.

"Mr. Quinn," a voice interrupted. "I'm Agent Dorsey, glad to finally meet you." The older man wore a dark suit and his shoes shined brighter than his bald head. Quinn shook his hand.

"I'm not sure why you want me here. To be honest, this is too personal for me to be involved." Quinn said frankly. Dorsey nodded to Casey, her clue to leave.

"I'll stop in and see Nelly tonight, discuss releasing things to the family. See you soon Quinn," Casey said and returned to her duty. There would be a second funeral, a second mourning. His stomach curled at the thought.

"Mr. Quinn, you found them," Dorsey said in a slow precise northern tone as he motioned around the room. "You are connected to one of them. And there are other matters we need to discuss considering your background. Come with me."

His background. Quinn liked to think his background resembled a man who did his job well. He followed the agent into a back room where maps and pictures flooded two full walls. Quinn removed his hat and stared at an aerial photo of Bear Claw Mountain. The lodge to the left, cliffs and meadows filling the largest part, and a small figure dressed in red crossing the driveway. Squinting, Quinn noted it was Nelly, possibly walking to the mailbox. She often wore that red coat everywhere.

"What can you tell me about Dermestid Beetles?" Dorsey asked. It wasn't a question Quinn expected. He thought he was asked here to talk about the past, maybe some minute-by-minute details of Sam's time in the underground room, not in a professional manner. This was an easier conversation.

"Some conservation departments use them instead of harsh chemicals in cases when a poached animal is slightly decomposed. The beetles are used to clean the flesh so we can investigate the bones for evidence of an arrow or bullet." Quinn's answer was professional but his mind was piecing clues together on why the FBI was asking him such a question they could get answers to easily. Worse, that they believed the killer used insects as part of his process. Agitation shifted to unease. "That's what was up there, skin beetles," he muttered out loud.

"Are you questioning me as a suspect Dorsey?" Just what he needed, a bunch of suits wasting time looking in the wrong direction instead of looking for a man capable of murder.

Dorsey crossed his arms, leaned on his desk. "You are a nice-looking man with a good job. Yet, you're single and have been most all your life. You were in a college dorm the night Becky Quinn, your cousin, disappeared, but you have a job that allows you to travel the state freely. Your home is simple," Dorsey scoffed and pushed off the desk. "Not a picture on the wall and only a loaf of bread and moldy ham in your fridge."

"You went through my house!" Quinn spoke up defensively. It wasn't like he had anything to hide, but to have his life dissected and sifted through, considered a person of interest, riled him.

"And your background," Dorsey continued. "The sheriff vouches for ya, but I suspect he would do the same for anyone in his town." Yes, the agent was fishing. Quinn hoped he would just turn that tactic onto a larger watering hole.

"I'm single because life threw me a curve. My house is a place to sleep, not a home. My every day is logged in with my corporal." Quinn stepped closer, looked down at the agent, daring him to proceed. "And if you dare to accuse me of capable of hurting my own flesh you might want to get one of your buddies in here because you will be picking yourself up off the floor for such an insult." Fury burned straight to his bones. "Profile someone capable of doing that," his voice raised and he pointed to the maps on the wall.

Dorsey laughed and took a step back. "I don't think you're guilty of anything, just doing my job before moving forward. You have a clean record. A bit solitary and sad, but an impressive one actually." He lifted a stack of papers, waved them in the air towards Quinn, and then dropped them back on the desk. "The sheriff seems to think your lone man status is honorable and your senior corporal *does* keep very good records, and was more than happy to share how compliant you would be offering us your services as well." That was just a kick to the head, Quinn seethed.

"We have so little to go on to be honest," Dorsey lifted a couple clear bags and shook them in the air. "Yellow paint chips, bugs, a few hairs that most likely belong to our victims. Nothing to point us in the right direction. What we need is fresh eyes that know the area, the people, and understand how to follow protocol." Dorsey turned and motioned to the large map with red and black lines, circles, and names. "Look at all of this and tell me what you see. A pattern, an idea, a thought?"

"I'm not a detective," Quinn remained steadfast in the center of the room. He didn't' want to know more. More meant he would know just what his thirteen-year-old cousin endured.

"You're trained to track down, follow leads, and investigate. You're more qualified than the sheriff and his deputies. We have identified more than a dozen women so far. They deserve our best, Warden." With that, Quinn surrendered. Becky wasn't the only victim.

He joined Dorsey as all the reasons he didn't want to be here, turned into the very reasons he needed to be.

"Here Dana Bloom was abducted from her home in Greenup. She was fourteen. When we contacted her family we discovered her mother was born here." Quinn lifted a brow and narrowed his gaze on the map.

"Here," Dorsey put a finger on a red x in the next county. "Jasmine Jackson, 17, was swimming with friends at a nearby lake. Just vanished after saying she was going to the restroom." Dorsey continued moving his finger over the map of northeastern Kentucky and connecting states, giving names to the red x's. "Carol Evans, 15, from Peebles, Ohio. Sillia Groves, 22, Manchester, Ohio. Kelsy Flora, 32, a daycare owner just a town from here," Dorsey stabbed at the map.

"So he *could* be local, keeps a small territory," Quinn muttered, collecting his own clues.

"Yes, he could. We have Dawn Johnson, 19, a suspected runaway from Maysville. Abbie Shrock, 20, a student from Morehead State University. Then there is Hannah Green, West Virginia student, 21. We have hundreds of pages of reports, attempted abductions, and suspicious activities to sift through. My team is working hard and fast." Dorsey sighed. It was clear this wasn't just a few victims sharing Becky's fate, but a small part of something Sam could have never predicted when she spotted the first glint of ivory.

"Any pattern? They're all different ages," Quinn continued to absorb what they knew so far. "Do they look alike or something? I mean my experience of this sort of things stops at late night television." He was getting a crash course in serial behavior whether he wanted it or not.

"Nothing concrete," Dorsey replied. "Not a one alike. In fact, each is very different. We need to match more identities with missing person reports for a better timeline, but we are confident he's taken one girl a year and each year the victim gets older." That sounded ridiculous to Quinn. Sensing his skepticism, Dorsey added. "It may be a new kind of pattern, but a pattern none the less. I'm bringing in a profiler to help sift through my theory."

"Wait, Becky was only thirteen when she disappeared," That meant…

"We do believe her the first. We're waiting for confirmation on that once we have all the identities, and that's why you're involved. You know the family, her routines, and seem to know her best friend pretty good from what I hear." Dorsey said with a bemused brow. Just how much of his personal life had Ron shared with this stranger?

"We can work every angle as information comes in, keep your sheriff in the loop, but you know a lot of people who are capable of taking a life." Dorsey lifted a brow. "Some out of season like those Everett's sheriff has locked up." His eyes returned to a scatter of pictures on the wall, settling on one shadowy one taken inside the underground room.

"He is a killer. He's careful. Nothing in that room indicates the victims died there. It's his trophy case,"

Quinn winced. "Trophies," Quinn tightened his fist at his side. He had dealt with plenty of trophy hunters in his life, but not at this measure.

"Sorry, but as hard as it is to hear, it's what killers do, they take trophies, mementos. Something to…remind them. Our man keeps them all together for some reason we can't figure out yet," Dorsey clasped Quinn's shoulder. "But we will. Our profiler is good and has been on multiple cases," he said with added assurance. "I need you to talk to Becky's friends, family. No one here wants to cooperate with us. Most I assume because to them, they feel they went through this already but you and I know we have to talk to everyone. Oh and one more thing,"

"Just one," Quinn smarted, his head reeling with the load of information. This was a lot to take in and it was personal. The man who sat center of these photos and red x's, had taken what was his.

"Who else in your line of work could get their hands on Dermestid Beetles?"

"We have a couple more wardens nearby, just a few counties from here. Another four guys further south I worked with when I started out. My corporal can give you a list, but most of them I feel I know fairly well. We aren't in the business of taking life, but protecting it." Quinn removed his cap and run his fingers through his hair.

"Everyone's a suspect Quinn. Remember that if you want to find the man who did this to them, to her." Dorsey had him now and Quinn couldn't deny it.

"Taxidermists use them too," Quinn quickly added now, remembering his past dealings and random license checks. "We do have an older man towards Rushing who does that sort of thing. There's another guy over in Lewis too. I can get you his name and address. I don't see either doing what you are suggesting though." Quinn didn't need to hear Dorsey explain what the FBI suspected. That their killer abducted girls, killed them at one location, and to hide evidence, let nature clean up the mess before he added them to his trophy room. This was not the sort of thing he imagined when he followed in his father's footsteps. This was sickening thriller novel turned into reality.

"You get me that list and I'll have the guys search every taxidermist in a two-hundred-mile radius of here and find out who sells these bugs, where they come from, and who's buying them."

"Well, they are natural to the surroundings. Why buy them if you can catch them for free," Quinn said. Dorsey scratched his chin, another angle to consider. Quinn thought that more common sense than leaving a trail.

"Why indeed. Our man could be frugal as well as smart. I think you're going to bring a lot more to this case than you think."

He took a seat on the long bench just as he did every day at this hour and pulled his evening supper out of his cooler. Stopping in at the little diner up north was worth the trip so far out of his comfort zone. Between the thick beef stew and fresh rolls and that ditsy waitress, he figured he would stop in again. She was thirty-two, and that's why he flirted, got her number.

These days the internet was the place to search. Women who seemed to hate mentioning their ages did so on social media like it was a responsibility, whereas when you asked a woman you would get a grunt or lie out of pursed lips. Not Shelly, sweet Shelly in her waitress green dress and creamy flesh. That woman had legs on her that was for sure. It didn't matter that her honey-colored hair came from a bottle. No it didn't matter at all when she blurted it out her age as if he asked the question. Still, another thought niggled at him. He always thought of her when scouting, felt his blood just warm knowing time was closing for that next thrill, so Shelly could be a substitute, a long-distance study, or maybe it was time to stop putting off the inevitable.

Freddie and Darion walked in and took a seat, pulling out their own suppers packed by dutiful wives. He didn't need a wife. Women were too much trouble. He only needed the fix, his reward for patience. Indulging once a year was safe, responsible, and didn't attract attention. It was a matter of control and control was key.

"Bad deal about the Quinn woman," Bob said as he pulled a foot long sandwich with all the fixings out of his lunch pack. Bob had a nagging wife, a son who just joined the police force, and a laid back way about him that was worthy of admiration.

"Who, Nelly?" Freddie asked with a mouth full. Most here were locals. Another reason he had learned to up his game, traveled further, used different methods to decide his victims. He had pilfered for two decades and no one was the wiser.

"No the younger one. Wife called at lunch in a hissy fit over it. Said when we got off shift to expect running into a lot of outsiders again," Bob shook his head. "I wish they would just stay out of our little town, leave those Quinn's be."

He did the mental math in his head. It was not the anniversary of his first love, the one that started it all, so why would outsiders be flooding Milford again. "What happened?" he asked biting into his yeast roll.

"Where have you been," Bob grilled, bumping his shoulder. "If you spent more time at home you would know our little town is being taken over by the feds and news crews."

That got his full attention. Maybe he should have spent less time studying Shelley and more time staying in the know of his own territory. A rookie mistake and here he had prided himself on being a veteran. A maven, a master, without so much as a glance his way. He could write a book, one that would only be read after he died of old age with a snarky grin on his wrinkled lips. The world would know just how stupid it was compared to him.

Right under their noses for years, he silently said.

"That Quinn, the one who runs that little hunting outfit, was up on Bear Claw and got herself hurt."

"Really?" He hated to hear that and hoped it was nothing serious. Beauty like that…it would be a shame to mar it.

"Yep, she fell in some sort of hole in the ground and got herself all busted up. They had search and rescue out all night before finding her. She's lucky she didn't freeze to death." Bob shook his head.

"Probably a sink hole," he said knowing the farm was littered with them. He spooned another bit of stew in his mouth though his appetite was now completing gone. Had his butterfly indeed been marred?

Blend in. Be normal.

"I heard that redbone hound of Clay's and the game warden found her," Twenty-four-year-old Darion Brooks added. Bob leaned forward at the new hire.

"Of course he did, and moved back into the lodge too. That man has had it bad for Dale's widow for a spell." Bob said then leaned back. "She already had worse. Quinn would make her a good one." It was no secret to anyone over the age of thirty that the local game warden had pined for years for that one. Such a shame he would never have her. A grin tried to split his face but he reined it in soldierly.

"I thought they were family?" Darion cringed then continued to munch on his soggy sandwich consisting of mostly bread and cheese.

"Samantha was married to Nelly's oldest boy, Dale. Quinn's the nephew. Lives over in Lewis now, if that's what you call it. Place looks like an abandoned house. Boy spends more time here than there." Bob took another bite, chewed as they all grew silent. "Alex told the wife she's healing. I can't see how after falling sixteen feet."

"Sixteen feet?" The exact distance he purposefully forged out himself. He didn't like coincidences.

"And on that side of the mountain. No sink holes up at the Chairs that I know of," Bob said, giving him a suspicious glance.

His heart hammered in his chest. *It couldn't be. I was so careful.* No way had his secret place had been found. But they mentioned the feds. *Feds taking over the town.* It took all his strength to rein in a yell. He recapped the plastic soup container before he squeezed it to death, put it back in his lunch cooler, and gripped his hands tightly together for composure. Blending in had come easy, but hearing in slow motion that your life's work, your private secrets were now possibly exposed, he hadn't a clue if he could remain on this bench much longer being just like the losers about him. Normal.

"Rumor is they found a bunch of dead bodies in a cave. Must be something to it to draw so much attention."

Those last words Bob spoke were sharper than blades to his own flesh. It was happening. His worst fear. Bob wasn't a gossip. Samantha Quinn had fallen through the old door he had kept under a layer of earth, leaves, and sticks for two decades. Samantha Quinn had found his den, his personal things, and the little troublemaker who had slipped through his fingers twenty years ago, had found his door, opened it, and walked right in. There was some irony there, but he'd address that later, when it could be amusing.

"Well come on boys, supper's over. A couple more hours and we get a couple days off. Say buddy, you really should do something about that moth problem of yours."

"I don't have a moth problem." He growled.

"Every time I see you," Bob yanked on his cotton shirt. "You got a hole in your shirt. For someone who can't stand a speck of dirt you sure look homely."

CHAPTER TWELVE

Thursday morning came calling and the next clients were due by early afternoon. Sam slipped outside, wanting just a minute to herself before life shifted again. They all had muddled through opening weekend, she and Quinn skirting around each other like strangers. She just didn't know how to act now. The Quinn she thought she knew didn't seem to be the one living under the same roof as her currently.

He had did as he said he would, hauled clients out in the early morning, patted them on the back proudly for a good hunt, and hauled them back. He made it look easy, like one didn't need years to know how to be a good hunting guide. That barbed her the most.

Each morning the house woke at five, a hearty meal served to eager men ready to fill their expensive out of state hunting tags. The three men from Georgia paid handsomely to have the first weekend, the most sought after of the entire season. Sam mingled lightly, presented pictures of some of the more sought after bucks she had fed all year, from their velvety first pics of summer, to the giants they grew into. She had a few antler sheds to tease their eagerness, and on Sunday, Sam congratulated all three men on their successful hunt, despite jealousy souring her gut for not being there, recording the moments they sighted their trophy, made a clean shot, and the adrenaline that followed when success was realized.

She looked up to her mountain. Hulk still roamed out there along with a few other young bucks that managed to elude hunters for now. She imagined him watching the three hunters climb into their Dodge and leave with a grin on his face. But Hulk wasn't alone up there, not now. It wasn't just his mountain, but now also belonged to a ghost.

She shivered in that recollection. She was off kilter, not just because of Quinn, but that five days ago she had discovered her best friend had been with her all along, buried in a room below the earth and trees she had walked over a thousand times. She gathered her faded sweater, pulled it into a hug. The outside dulled. Bare trees were shadowed in a grey sky. Death had tainted everything once more.

Connie had been over twice, checking in as friends do. Wednesday morning headlines had everyone rattled. It was all happening again, only this time Sam wasn't a child, afraid and wishing she had done different, but the fresh stab still pierced and bled.

Nelly would have to face the media soon, they all knew, and after that article, How Many Victims Are Hidden on Bear Claw Mountain, it was inevitable. Sam gritted her teeth wishing she could protect her from that. If the reporters did their jobs and looked back nineteen years to the girl and boy who tried to save their best friend, she and Jake would have to face them too.

She let out a puff of pinned up air. Cold and hot collided, forming a visible breath. She wasn't a child needing coddled, but she ached for arms to hold her and keep her balanced. A cry would do her good, Connie said. No, a cry would certainly do no one any good. Tears didn't change a thing. She straightened her shoulders. Whatever came, she would just have to shoulder it.

A few flurries danced about. The turning of the season was a time when she usually felt her most alive, but not this season. To think all this time, all the searching they had done, and she had been right here, waiting to be discovered. She was glad Becky had been found. Being lost was a terrible thing.

Sam closed her eyes and envisioned the long brown hair, Becky's signature beauty, and eyes that honestly lit up when she smiled. Did she know that they had become sisters, marriage ties binding them for eternity? Did she know what her mother had gone through, how she grieved and prayed desperately for her? Did she know she had a nephew with the same hair and sweetness she had? Sam liked to think so. She also liked to think all those talks on the mountain, the one-sided ones she had from the old stand, Becky heard too. Perhaps Becky had been the one listening. She clung to that and set aside the rest.

When afternoon arrived, Sam welcomed fresh guests with a smile. She knew Miken, Frank, and Greg Pollard, brothers from Ohio, but now she wished she hadn't scheduled so many this year.

And if Frank called her gimpy one more time she might just explode. The man joked innocently, but she wasn't up for foolish banter.

The Whitley's, from Utah, were a middle-aged couple, financially endowed, and bouncing to hunting preserves all over the country as a hobby. Sam figured Sean Whitley had more trophies on one wall then the Deer Creek Lodge had altogether, and after a brief conversation with his down to earth wife, Chrystal, she had guessed right. Sam listened to talk about extravagant hunts from Canada to Texas and beamed when Chrystal paid compliment to their cozy and welcoming lodge, claiming it was one of her favorites to visit.

When she helped serve supper, she could sense that Quinn watched her. He had spent the last four days helping Ron, and though he never spoke of it, Sam knew he was helping with the case of Becky's disappearance. She felt his gaze following here every move. She never liked such attention, but had to admit, she had been observing the man more over these last few days. He was different here. Not like the boy who left for college and a career that kept him away from his family. Connie accused her of wearing blinders all the time and Sam was discovering she may have been right about that.

Brody was another reason she paid close attention. Watching him wait by the window in the evenings for Quinn to return brought on a strange jealousy. One that grew the moment Quinn walked into the door wearing a grin as wide as her clients and her son bounced into his arms. Brody clung to Quinn and listened to every retelling of the two clean kills opening day had delivered. Sunday it took all the strength Sam had to hold back tears when Brody wanted Quinn to tuck him in and not her that night.

Had she not been the sole recipient of Brody's affection? Was it selfish to hate being so looked over instead of happy her son was getting attention owed him?

What would Becky say to her selfish thoughts? Sam quickly shook off thinking of her and how long she had waited to be found. She had suffered that grief long ago, let it create in her an over-protectiveness with Brody some called helicopter parenting.

Quinn grunted, his gaze traveling to her leg. If he was going to say something about her ditching the crutches after only ten days, she'd already practiced how to remind him *she* was none of his concern. She shot a glare over one shoulder but his intense stare had her faltering again. Quickly turning away, she didn't miss the low chuckle of his timbre tone.

"I know you men are eager to explore the area, pick your spots as Sam calls it," Nelly shot her a grin. "But tomorrow night the local church is having a fundraiser in town. We have one every year. Craft booths early in the day if you ladies want to come while the men are out?" Nelly lifted a bowl of steamed broccoli and carted it to the table.

"That's sounds nice," Chrystal replied already digging in to her full plate like she hadn't eaten in days. It was a miracle she was so trim with such an appetite.

"We have some of the best BBQ you'll ever eat. All the money goes to charity, which this year happens to be our local hospital. There's dancing too."

"Sounds wonderful. Will you *all* be going?" Jillian Crest, the Florida beauty, asked as she toyed with her plate. With a waist that size, Sam was surprised she dared to nibble at a roll and ignore vegetables like a child.

Sam had never really given much thought to her weight. Not as she had years ago after having Brody and suspecting her husband's trips to town to hang with the guys was something worry worthy. She hated to admit she worked hard to look her best for him then. She hated it more that all that work hadn't paid off. She couldn't compete with real beauty, and finally stopped trying to.

"We do. Most all of the town does. In the past our clients have attended and enjoyed it," Nelly added. The meal went on in cadence. Sam listened with both ears, served seconds when asked, and nudged Brody more than a couple times to finish his plate.

"So I hear you are a law enforcement officer Mr. Quinn," Jillian asked not so subtly. It was clear she had no problem sizing Quinn up from head to boot despite the large rock on her ring finger. James Crest was either oblivious, or accustomed to his wife's flirtations.

"I'm a warden with Kentucky Fish and Game," Quinn replied. Sam cleared her plate and went to retrieve dessert. The faster the meal was over with the quicker she could curl back under the covers and mark this day over.

"My boy is helping while he's off work, so my daughter-in-law can rest her knee." Sam almost dropped the apple pie she plucked from the counter to serve at Nelly's unexpected insinuation that Quinn was her child, and she, his bride. Of course the Florida beauty was flirting, that was apparent, but to toss her under the bus, paint a picture of fabrication, caught Sam off guard.

"How sweet of you. Your job sounds dangerously intriguing," Jillian continued unaffected by Nelly's subtle warning. Sam was surprised to find that bothered her even more than Nelly's remark. Some women simply turned the stomach sour.

"We have pie everyone; apple, pumpkin, and berry." Sam interrupted a little too loudly. Quinn scooted back his chair and rose to relieve her of her handful, his fingers barely grazing hers. She didn't need his help and pushed aside the unexpected delight of his touch racing over her flesh. Pretending was a skill she had mastered. Training only increased her talent to be separate from the incident.

Until now.

He smelled good. When he quirked a smile that melted butter and made sure eye contact was made before turning away she bit into her tongue. Quinn was a flirt by reputation, and she'd head well to remember that. Being a lonely widow made for lasting mistakes, and Sam didn't like mistakes.

"Few things I like better than pie," Quinn said. Jillian batted her eyes his way. Sam resisted the urge to harrumph out loud. *Typical.* "Oh Sam, you forgot a knife, dear" Quinn said mockingly. She gritted her teeth and limped back to the utensil drawer. When she returned she slammed it down on the table beside him hard enough to catch his attention.

Brandon and Sophia Walker, a couple from Minnesota, both jerked apart. They couldn't have been married more than a year, Sam guessed. The way they necked, and floated smiles at one another, said they hadn't had the time yet to move on past the happy first stages.

"Samantha, those pics you sent where amazing. I'm hoping you put me in line with Hulk or maybe Prince. Both look like massive bucks that could score at least 180." Greg was the eldest of the Pollard brothers. This was their third trip to Deer Creek Lodge and they knew all too well that she was a widow. Sam suspected before the weekend was over, Greg would try another of his attempts to have her join him for dinner.

Brushing off her reaction to Quinn, Sam returned to the table and gave Greg her full attention. He was a nice-looking man. Brown hair, blue eyes, with a smile that looked like something he had well-tuned over the years but wasn't really his own. Last year he took rejection well, understood her personal stance to not date clients, but the way he watched her tonight told her that he was hoping she'd changed her mind since last year. She hadn't.

"Sam won't be taking you out this weekend. I will," Quinn said with a hint of authority. "Clark Quinn, the guide you met last year, will be here in the morning to help too." Quinn offered him a slice of apple pie and grinned mischievously.

"I wish *you* were fit to take us out this year. Sorry about the leg. How did you hurt it?" Greg lifted a brow to Sam. Greg Pollard was down to earth, simple, and apparently didn't read, newspapers or internet. Headlines were buzzing about the nineteen-year-old cold case and mass grave site nearby. One even pictured Becky at thirteen-years-old, next to eighteen-year-old Emily Walker from Ohio.

"Mom fell in a big hole on the mountain," Brody shot out as kids tended to do. Sam floated him a soft look and pointed to his plate again.

"Sorry to hear it." He offered a sorrowful smile, but his blue lake gaze drifted along her five foot seven inch frame. Yeah, he would ask her out again for sure. She hadn't dated since Dale, and that was in high school. Did people just go out for dinner, enjoy each other's company or was more expected. She hadn't a clue what adults did on Saturday night dates anymore. All she knew was after putting a seven-year-old to bed she watched movies, ate ice cream, and made it to bed before eleven. And that was a treat if she wasn't off working the night shift.

Quinn got to his feet, scraping his chair loudly across the wooden floor, and began clearing the table. It was a rude gesture.

"No worries Mr. Walker. Henry here grew up on this farm. He knows what he's doing." Nelly assured.

"Sam, I think Brody is about to fall asleep in his plate," Quinn said in a sour tone. "Might want to take him on up." Noting that he was indeed right about her son dozing off, she stood, collecting her plate and limping it to the sink. She could see his face was pinched, brows gathered in an angry v, and locked gazes with him. "You can turn in too, I'll see to the guests tonight." It sounded more like an order than a suggestion. She didn't want to cause a scene in front of clients and figured he would use that against her too.

"Fine," she snapped. "I'll just pick him up and carry him upstairs. Or..." Sam turned to asked for assistance. Two could play that game, she thought. Before she could act on it, Quinn gripped her arm. It was firm but not altogether threatening.

"I'll carry him, if you follow." His eyes narrowed on her.

"You're being ridiculous." She pulled away slowly and lifted her chin. "I'll lead," she stormed off.

In Brody's room Sam worked calming her temper as she heard his footsteps climb the stairs. "Stubborn man," she quipped turning on the bedside lamp and turned down the bed.

"More rare than a stubborn female." Sam jolted upward as he stepped into the room, Brody drifting contently in his arms. She took two steps back as he laid her son down and began removing his shoes.

"It's been a lot of years since I was given a curfew. You were rude to one of my clients."

"He was hitting on you."

"And batting eyes with the married Jillian was more appropriate than an unwed man hitting on me." She kept her voice low but made sure to put some flare in it. Quinn stood, steadily and put Brody's shoes near the door before closing in on her.

"I don't flirt with married women," Quinn said angrily.

"Since when haven't you? Don't play innocent with me." He flinched. Why did he flinch? When he marched to her, Sam retreated instinctually. She had gone too far, but for the life of her he needed to mind his own business and stop treating her like a little sister needing looked over. She swallowed hard. She thought Quinn anything but a brother, but he didn't need to know that.

"If I ever crossed a line like that, only you would know." But she did. Dale told her all about his fling years ago.

"You come in here, take over, winning hearts despite being a complete chauvinist jerk. I'm not your blood, you can't boss me around, send me to bed at eight like a toddler," she lifted a finger in full fury now. "And if some guy wants to flirt with me, he can. That's none of your business Henry."

"It *is* my business and am very aware you're not blood." The timbered sound of his voice caused her to tremble. He was too close. She took another step back but that was as far as she could go.

"Okay, then." She lifted her chin, pretended she didn't sound utterly stupid and childish, and planted her fist on her hips. "We don't even like each other," her voice had gone weak, and she hated the quiver in her tone. "Just stay out of my way and I will stay out of yours."

His smile came slow and careful, crept unhurried across his rugged face. Sam wondered what it would feel like to brush her fingers through his beard, then shook off the thought as quick as it came. What was wrong with her? Determined to stand her ground, Sam met his gaze on equally. This man would not upend her this time.

Quinn lifted a hand, brushed her hair behind her ear, and she was certain he felt her tremble. "That's impossible," he muttered. Onyx eyes stared hungrily at her mouth and her head pounded with the wild rhythm of her own heartbeat.

"I hate men looking at you." His eyes lifted and nothing in them said, charming, but ruthless, determined. Her stomach quaked and all she could do was stand there, motionless. "Good night Samantha."

He stepped away, leaving in the same cool manner as when he walked in. She listened to his footsteps descend the stairs, but she hadn't moved from Brody's wall where she only now realized Quinn backed her in to. It was clear her night would be filled with nightmares full of bones and haunting memories, but before sunrise, they might just turn into dreams.

CHAPTER THIRTEEN

After Brody's play, Sam followed her son into the old church hall. Wired on sweets and a job well-done, Brody insisted on keeping on his pilgrim costume for the rest of the festivities.

The vast room had old tile floors and cream painted walls that carried an echo from every sound, but it kept out the cold and could hold more than a few hundred souls without stepping on each other. Brody held her hand, pulling her along. Since Quinn had given him the job of watching over her, her son did not disappoint. The bulk of her wrap was visible under the hem of her blue dress. Her doctor said nothing to her for refusing to wear the pesky knee brace, and she'd freed herself of that hindrance.

It didn't seem right to have the fundraiser. Not with the recovery efforts on the mountain, but as Nelly insisted, life went on without needing permission. A fact Sam was fully aware of. Milford had become the center of the country. Murders, serial killers, and mass graves, marring its otherwise hidden beauty. She noted the sheriff speaking with a well-dressed stranger. The camera man beside her told this was no visitor but yet another vulture hoping for a claim of something to spur her career forward. Sam moved right, close to the drink table hoping to avoid her.

It was easy to avoid calls when the answering machine could handle that job well enough. Quinn had taken over collecting the daily mail. Sam knew he did it to censor it more than anything for Nelly's sake, but here in the public they had no defenses against questions and news. Maybe she should find Nelly, sidle close. Sam could step in line if necessary. Nelly didn't need this again, not after all her hard work for this event.

It didn't take long to spot her mother-in-law. Nelly didn't look like a grieving mother in Quinn's strong arms, but a woman enjoying a dance. Sam smiled at the sweet sight of them. He really could be a good guy. Dale had painted a picture in her head of a different man and for years it was hard seeing Quinn any other way. It didn't make sense though. Dale loved him. You don't lie about the people you love.

"Glad to see you two finally getting along. It's been a long time coming." Connie stepped beside her and filled two cups with punch. Sam pulled her gaze from the dance floor.

"Mom, can I go play with Charlie?" Brody asked. She nodded and watched him run off towards Charlie and his father. Charlie's father threw up a hand. He was safe with Caleb and boys should not carry the worries of adults.

"We tolerate each other. That's all," Sam said. She accepted the cup and took a sip of the tangy concoction. "He did see Brody's play, though he missed the last two years of them."

"It's a start I guess." They both watched Tim Grimes stroll into the room. His once large frame had added a few more pounds, a poor posture, and a wicked habit of tugging his jeans nervously. The man was a puppy, harmless, always searching for affection. At least once a year Sam had to let him down. Today's target was Sheryl Mawk a part-time dispatcher and half Tim's age. Sam almost pitied Tim when rejection came, but if rumors were half right, Jake was keeping the twenty-six-year-old Sheryl in his sights. They had been seen out more than once recently.

"But if you ever paid attention, you'd know he's never missed a one of Brody's plays," Connie said. "Why do you hate him?"

"Quinn attended the Thanksgiving plays?" Sam flinched but quickly collected herself on the new fact. "Well, he's a jerk, a womanizer," she smarted. "And he had never approved of me. Dale used to tell me how he begged him not to marry me. How we weren't fitted." Sam huffed. "Once he told Dale he was better off to leave me. Can you believe that?" That jab still hurt.

"Sure doesn't look like a man who disapproves of you at all. In fact, I don't ever remember a time Quinn wasn't into you." Connie smirked.

"That's ridiculous." She looked out again just as Quinn looked her way. There was a time she had thought so too, but she learned how wrong that was.

"He just likes flirting and chasing what isn't his. Dale told me everything. You should have seen him with one of my client's wives then had the nerve to flirt with me. The man has no boundaries."

"You're not seeing straight, and always did believe Dale more honorable than he was." Connie said pointy.

"That's not fair." Sam argued.

"No its not and I'm sorry, but we both know Quinn is a great guy. Sometimes when you talk about him I can't tell if you're talking about Quinn or Dale to tell the truth. I have known them both all their lives and have never known Quinn to be what you think he is. In fact, no one thinks of him that way...but you."

Sam wasn't sure how to respond to that.

"Sure he's handsome, dated a few ladies, and yet, has never settled down." Connie looked towards Quinn and Nelly on the dance floor. "I ask myself, is that because he wants a life as a lonely bachelor or is it that Quinn hasn't found what he has always wanted?" She turned back to Sam. "I believe the latter, and wish you would stop being so hard on the man."

"Well, who spiked your punch with a lemon?"

Connie touched her arm. "I love you Sam, like a sister, that's why I am saying this to you now. You've let Dale's lies, and the guilt you carry because of his death, cloud your judgment. For a woman capable of putting out fires and calming hysterics, you're a bit stupid when it comes to matters of the heart. Are you afraid?"

"Afraid? I show my face in this town even knowing the whispers about the poor widow who wasn't good enough to keep her husband satisfied. You fuss that I should go out, date, well I don't see a line forming to ask me." Sam waved an arm.

"Few would dare ask you because they know you'll say no." Connie had a point. "You're hiding behind that little excuse. You're afraid to trust another man with your heart, and if I may be bold here,"

"By all means don't stop now," Sam smarted. She had always admired Connie's forwardness, but not when it was aimed straight at her.

"You're afraid to discover all you think you know is a lie. You're afraid to give your heart to someone because you expect them to hurt it. If you think Henry is a flirt, a scoundrel," her voice lowered to a southern draw, "Ask him. That man would never lie to you." Connie strolled off leaving Sam momentarily stunned.

"Sam, how are you?" Sam spun around and pasted on a quick smile for Ed Zimmerman. Surely Connie's words had left her scowling. Ed had grown out of that awkward high schooler with too many books and glasses into a fine dressed banker who lost the glasses, replaced them with contacts, and took running very seriously. Sam always gave him a wave if she saw him running outside of town when she was heading home from her shift.

"I'm good. Healing nicely," she said when he looked at her leg.

"I'm sorry about that. Well, about all that's going on. It's horrible. It's good you're there with Nelly to help."

"I'm lucky to have her more than the other way around. She is tougher than she looks," They both watched as the sheriff guided Nelly on the dance floor next. A Black Hawke tune that Sam

Bones on the Mountain

figured could either be danced slow and close or apart began playing. Surprisingly the pair chose close.

"She also has a way about her to steal your heart." Sam pretended not to care which direction Quinn had run off too. It was none of her concern, just as she was none of his, but Connie may be right. Sam was afraid. Afraid Connie was right about her fear of trusting love again. Was it true that all the men in Milford thought her the forever widow? Well enough with that, she told herself.

"How about giving this old lab buddy a dance, if you're up to it with your leg and all. You might make me look good out there." Ed reached out and offered her his hand. Sam ignored the hand, and looped an arm into his. She quelled a laugh when she noted his chest swell as he guided her to the dance floor. Not all men where like Dale after all.

"Leg feels great and I think dancing is a good idea. Thank you for asking me."

As the song finished, Sam applauded the band, surprised how well they performed. The music faded from Rivalry to Lost in this Moment from Big and Rich. A little too romantic to be dancing with a friend, she mentally noted. But before she could excuse herself, Ed was pulling her back in for another dance. Sam caught a glimpse of Peter Richmond, an old classmate who drove a truck for a living like Tim did, walking their way. Okay, so she opened the gate and now it seemed she might be trampled on. Suddenly Peter stopped dead in his tracks. His eyes went from her to just beyond her before that frown deepened the curve of his untrimmed mustache. Turning on a heel, he strode back the way he came. Well, what ever had changed his direction, Sam was glad for it.

"Evening Ed," Quinn said and gripped Sam's hand, pulling her away and into his arms. What happened to "may I cut in?" Sam thought as his hand lay firmly on her lower back, urging distance from the local banker.

"Quinn, we were dancing," Ed said with more whine than temper.

"And now we are." He gave Sam a spin, lifting her from the floor as if she weighed nothing. In three smooth strides Ed was left behind. Over Quinn's shoulder she watched Ed plant two fist on his hips angrily. However, he didn't do anything to stop it.

When her feet touched the floor again, her head was spinning, but her temper was completely intact. "What are you doing?" She caught her breath and brushed her hands down her dress before he captured her again.

"Dancing," he answered casually. "What were you doing with Ed Zimmerman?"

"Whatever I want," she grinned, ignoring the fact Quinn held her a lot more possessively than Ed and his sweaty hands had. Quinn growled but said nothing to her comment. "This is not a 'do as I say not as I do' Quinn." Who did he think he was?

"Don't you have a date here, or someone you can pester?" Sam said as he pulled her closer. Surely they looked quite the spectacle for a church fundraiser. She would have a bruise come morning by the tight grip Quinn had on her waist.

"Nope, I'm all yours. To pester of course." He dipped his head teasingly.

"And every other woman's," she murmured.

"There's dealing with the female gender and then there's dealing with you," he countered but didn't loosen his grip.

"I assure you regardless of my lack of make-up and hair dye, I am female too." His gaze took its sweet time to explore that statement.

"You are all woman, no adornments needed to see that." His grip softened.

"That didn't feel like a compliment." She shrugged absent-mindedly letting him lead.

"You'd take a compliment and spit it in my face," he said moving a bit closer, eyes still dancing between anger and delight. "Want a compliment?" The corner of his mouth lifted into a smug grin.

"You might need your male ego stroked regularly but I don't require it," she turned to leave and he yanked her back hard enough this time she smacked into him. He raised a brow, dragging one side of his mouth with it.

"Song isn't over. How's the knee?"

"Fine," she said sharply, one hand resting on his shoulder, and the other fitting into his hand. If he made a scene, she would make him regret it. It was an awkward dance between two people who didn't know any of the steps.

"Brody made a good pilgrim," he said adding small talk. "Better than that pie costume Nelly stuffed him in last year." He chuckled and Sam felt Connie's last sting pierce her again. *So he had seen last year's Thanksgiving play.*

"Nelly likes to do things herself," was all she could say.

"So do you," he said in a low voice but she heard every syllable. They danced for a moment in silence, his arms holding her, his feet guiding her. Slowly his head leaned in until the sides of their faces almost touched. The scent of his soap, his clothes, filled her senses. She held her tongue, as did he, for a moment, a moment that felt like their truce had been reclaimed and something else was being sprouted. His face, mere inches from her own, whispered another breath on her skin.

"We've never danced before." She wished he would stop teasing her flesh like that. Eyes floated their way, and when Connie and Matt smiled like two cats with mouths full of canary, Sam realized how it might look. She had finally gotten through the first round of rumors and wasn't about to endure a new scandal with her name attached. She could date, enjoy the company of a man, just not this one regardless how safe and warm and wonderful he felt.

"People are staring."

"That's because you look beautiful, and people have always stared at you Samantha." His charm was boiling over. How long had he wanted to get her in his arms? It was time he started using his heart instead of his head. It was hers already.

"You two look so lovely," Chrystal muttered as she and her husband danced nearby.

"Oh we," Sam started to explain. Nelly may have started painting that picture but Sam was making it look better.

"Thank you Mrs. Whitley. She makes me look good," Quinn grinned and gave Sam a casual twirl. She was lovely, so lovely. How many dances had he missed in trying to be the good guy.

"See. Now people are gonna think..."

"That I am dancing with the most beautiful woman in the room. I thought the red-wine dress was killer, but I must admit, blue suits you too." He had maimed her speechless again, and that sent an unexpected thrill through him. His boldness grew as the song continued and his arms still held her. Quinn brushed a finger over her hair and slid to the pulse racing in her neck. He felt every thrashing beat against his fingertips.

"I'm not your type. Don't waste your charms." Her body was reaching perilously close to panic.

"I'm not a wasteful man and I've only ever had...one type."

She had to know.

"You shouldn't say such things," she stuttered and a soft warm shade of strawberry climbed over her high cheekbones.

"I should have said them sooner," he admitted. He watched her inner struggle. Dale had painted an ugly portrait of him, and he couldn't blame her for being cautious. Dale had deceived her for years, used Quinn to hide his own digressions. He would give her time, let it all come on slowly.

"May I ask you something?" she bit her lip and focused on her steps.

"You can ask me anything." He would not lie to her, even if she might not like what his answers.

"That night he came home with a busted lip and bloody nose, he said it was from defending you." Quinn hadn't a clue what tale Dale conjured up there, but remembered well the night he found him with another woman at the Brick. "I hated you for that." She was tough, and didn't hold back. It was that toughness that got her through this far.

"I've never done anything that needed defending." He said without flinching. She studied him intently and when awareness came, he saw that too. He was glad she was coming to know him, the real him, and not the one Dale spoke of. It was a start, Quinn measured. "You did that to him?"

"Needed done," he replied guiltless. "Some men take for granted what they have and they shouldn't without having a reminder of it." He never regretted the punch, the warning he served with it. Quinn's only regret was that he and Dale hadn't made amends before time run out. He had no intentions of letting time get past him again.

"Did you do it, for…"

"I did." He quickly answered. He did it for her. Everything, his whole lonely existed, had been for her.

"Then I won't hate you for that anymore."

"It's a start Sam." He whispered and pulled her close again.

"Quinn, I think we are drawing a crowd." He looked about at all the faces pointed their way.

"We could shut them all up, right now," he leaned close, a breath away, watched uncertainty riddle her expression. "Or," he moved back, still holding her firmly in his hand. "We can let them wonder a while longer." Her mouth fell open at the idea. She struggled between nerves, irritation, and bewilderment, all fascinating sensations that had a way of driving a heart equally mad.

"What will it be Samantha, now or later?" For a second Sam had to think about that, but just a quick second, lasting less than a good blink before stepping out of his arms. Sensing her unease, Quinn let her go this time. He had put a lot on her tonight and she had already endured plenty in the past few days.

"We have guest and an early morning. I should go fetch Brody and get home."

CHAPTER FOURTEEN

A starless sky and a hidden moon gave her nothing to stare at out her window. Restlessness getting the better of her, Sam listened every time the front door opened and closed with unexplainable interest. Currently she could hear Sophia giggle as Brandon chased her up the stairs. Who would have thought two people could turn a hunting trip into a romantic adventure. She rolled her eyes and continued rearranging her closet, by seasons rather than color made more sense anyways.

Nelly was currently slumbering downstairs. After a night of dancing, and to Sam's surprise, a ride home in the sheriff's patrol vehicle, she had finally worn out. Sam had watched from her upper bedroom window as Ron opened Nelly's door, walked her to the house like a man who knew how to treat an interest. It was sweet to think Nelly might find love again.

Bones on the Mountain

Seething, Sam ripped the dress she had worn the night Connie had tricked her into showing up at the Brick from the hanger. Who cared if Quinn was still not back? He could have been called out on duty perhaps, or simply decided to sleep under another roof tonight. It made no matter to her.

But it did, and that was the problem. She had pined over him as a girl, cried tears of heartbreak when her crush revealed itself for what it was, a crush. Too young to understand matters of the world the day they first met, and even now, womanhood was cruel, tempting the mind and body with racing sensations. Eyes didn't declare love, hands touching didn't mean the triggers they left upon the skin meant promises. Still, despite talking herself weary didn't stop the thought of Henry Quinn defending her.

At the click of a door close by, Sam slipped into the hallway. Dim light and moving shadows filtered out of Brody's bedroom. Alarmed, she moved towards it but stopped abruptly recognizing the strong silhouette standing at Brody's bed. He had come to say goodnight, again. Sam let out a frustrated breath. And Brody, was still awake. The little faker was getting good at playing dead lately. She could have sworn that third book did the job this time. Sam stepped back into the hall to conceal herself.

"I think your momma would rather you went on to sleep. You'll be a bear to wake for Nana's pancakes come morning." Quinn said. The sound of the mattress said he sat down.

"You didn't say goodnight," Brody said wearily, the same way he did anytime he fought sleep.

"I didn't, did I? Well, goodnight bub. Now go to sleep before you get us both in trouble." Brody giggled and Sam imagined Quinn tucking him in playfully.

"Henry. Can I tell you a secret," Brody asked and she leaned closer to hear.

"You can, only if you go to sleep." Quinn bargained. Sam couldn't help but grin. Brody had a way about him that would always get him what he wanted. She liked to think it was those deep blue eyes he had of hers, but in reality it was just his natural Quinn charm.

"I think I'm going to get married," Brody said with complete seriousness. Sam put her hand over her mouth to stifle a laugh. The things her son came up with.

"I'm not playing jokes Henry." Brody's voice hitched when Quinn chuckled too. "Bella Roberts and Charlie said everyone has to do it. It's the law you know?" Brody was confiding in Quinn, a man, and not her. A little jealousy pinged but she managed to not let it disturb her too much. Boys needed male figures, and between Quinn and her dad who seldom was about, it was all her son had.

"Is it now? I must have missed that one," Quinn added in a light tone. "Law number 177 it is."

"And you have to pick someone you love and it has to be forever with no take backs."

"No take backs. I like that. You got a girl in mind?" Quinn ventured. Maybe Quinn wasn't the best mentor in this department.

"Yep. I pick Nana. She says she loves me and I can have cookies any time I want. She even lets me get away with not washing my ears. She knows I hate that." Sam frowned. No more Nelly at bath time.

"Well, those are good reasons and fine qualities in a woman, but there's one problem with that bub." Sam smiled, touched by the connection between her son and Quinn. In truth, they had always been like that. If only she hadn't been so stubborn, bent on seeing one way instead the way he was.

"What's the problem?"

"She's kind of like.... my mother. Aunt Nelly raised me since I was smaller than you. She's the only mother I can ever remember having. So even though I call her Aunt Nelly, she's a mom, to me."

"What happened to your mom?" Sam should reveal herself, interrupt or something, but curiosity kept her feet planted. She knew the story but never had she ever recalled a time Quinn spoke of his parent's death. She couldn't blame him, seeing as she and her father had never spoken about her own mother.

"I lost my mom and my dad when I was a little, a little younger than you. They died in a car accident. I came to live here after that. In fact, this used to be my old room when I was your size."

"I lost my dad in an accident too." Brody said and Sam felt a tear threaten.

"I know bub. Your dad was a special guy. I know he loved you very much." Sam appreciated his kind words.

"Like Nana?"

"Just like that," Quinn said. "So you see that's why I don't think you shouldn't be marrying my mother. I'd like to keep her to myself a little longer." A long silence carried and Sam moved ever-so quietly to turn back to her own room.

"What if I let you marry my mom and that way I can marry yours?" No chuckle followed this time and Sam nearly tumbled over in her current awkward position. "We could have them for like… forever that way."

"Well now, that changes everything." His tone lifted and Sam could just imagine the arrogant smile on his face. Leave it to Quinn to turn her son's seriousness into a teasing matter. Sam straightened, crossing her arms, not liking how this conversation was going.

"Mom says sharing is what people should do." Brody put in for good measure.

"Your mother is a smart woman."

"Like Nana," Brody added.

"Yes, just like your grandmother."

"So, is it a deal? I marry Nana, you marry mommy. Everyone's happy and Bella and Charlie will still be my friends." Sam hung on those next words. She hadn't thought Brody capable of such thinking and yet understood the emptiness felt in the loss of a parent. Surely Quinn would set him straight. "And if you marry my mom you can be my dad. All the other kids have dads, so I will have one too."

The wind outside kicked up and the sound of old chimes batting together were all the sound in the world right now. What mother held tears in with words like that?

"I'd be honored Brody, to be both to you and your momma. So it's a deal, but under one condition. You're not old enough to marry just yet. So I get to go first. I've waited longer." Sam gasps. *To do what?*

As the light went out, she slithered back to retreat and almost stumbled, catching herself in the door frame with both hands. Quinn stepped into the hall, locking eyes with her immediately. He said nothing to the tears running down her face but she could read it troubled him by the way his black brows knitted together. Slowly recognition that she had heard their private and rather unexpected conversation registered and his guileless features softened.

"Goodnight Samantha," he nodded casually before walking to the forgotten room just down the hall.

Nothing felt more like a slap to the soul than returning home after days laboring and finding your life's work a mockery. He prepared himself accordingly, suspected some of what the guys mentioned, but to see strangers with cameras around their necks, the suits with hawk-like eyes sizing up every man, woman, and child in their range, twisted his insides into an array of knots. And now, as if nothing was wrong in the world, here was half the town laughing and dancing, mingling with outsiders, like nothing affected them at all.

He wasn't going to watch them all celebrate with their smiling teeth and wicked laughs after what they did. Had he not earned a place here? Was he too not one of them? For the first time since he turned eighteen and drove into the small town with no motel and more green than pavement, he felt like a stranger.

Kelly Simpson, the local florist who had been kind enough to give him work when he rolled into town on fumes, had been serving punch. Not once had she bothered to turn those green eyes his way. Had he not fixed her plumbing just last week, for free, and she dared snub him. Ed had brushed by him without a hello to spare. It seemed his eyes were set on Sam Quinn. He didn't blame him, and had to admit he was here for the same reason too. He had plans for her. Plans Ed should know not to mess with. Hadn't fate declared her his? She hadn't dated or let another into her heart since Dale. If that wasn't a sign of destiny he didn't know what was.

Dale, he thought as he watched Sam being swept off to the dance floor, her blue dress revealing a shapely form like water rippling over rock. That was unplanned, but if he knew she would be so compliant to his plans, be his muse for over two decades, unconscious or not, he would have cut that life short faster.

To be the best, one didn't waver from the process, but for her, it was a necessary risk.

He cringed to think of them sifting through his lair, exposing his darkest secrets. Standing there in the church hall just a couple hours earlier, he knew she hadn't meant to find his lair, but doing so, he did intend to make her pay for it. First he would admire her. He had a few more days before her special day to do so, and he would still be doing just that if the warden hadn't ruined that too. After all these years, the arrogant man finally straightened up, made his own move. She didn't look to object, and that burned him. This was not how it was supposed to be at all.

He carried the mixed gas jug, thick as sludge on the inside, and slipped into the barn still seething over the whole mess. How dare they take what wasn't theirs. His trophies, his work, all now being sifted over, cataloged, and numbered. They touched those hands, eyes that were his now saw them, watched them enter their sanctuary. Just as disturbing to imagine another touching *her*.

His throat singed at the injustice, threatened to deliver more, but he willed it down. They were gone, his beauties, and he couldn't get them back any more than he could start over, collect them all again. But he could have her, now. It was she that fed his appetite, taught him not to make mistakes. Yes, all was not lost once he had her.

Revenge wasn't his way, but right now he wasn't feeling very controlled. So revenge would feed his fury, that bone deep ache. Nothing he did tonight would be remembered, except by him. This was self-satisfaction. He deserved something after doing all the work.

His next DuPont shift started in two days. Plenty of time to observe, plan, and act. He'd have his prize. It would be torture, waiting another year. He shouldn't break routine, that's the kind of thing that drew attention, but that was before everything crumbled around him.

Tonight he would do this one thing to numb some of his hurt. He'd never go to The Chairs again, descend the steep bank where the ancient tree rooted. And now that he could never again sit with them, talk with them, fresh tears would fall for this town who thought him nothing but a mere shadow.

He could take what he wanted anytime he wanted. Always could.

He would rip out all their hearts…soon.

CHAPTER FIFTEEN

It made no sense, but after the setback of having not one side-by-side start this morning, Sam called Jake Foster just as Quinn asked her to do. Thankfully her clients were good sports that none of the utility vehicles were running at five thirty in the morning.

Sam saw to the dishes, and then set Brody up with a new puzzle. The kid loved solving things and his teacher recommended three hundred count was not out of his league at all. Sam slipped into her coat before marching out to the old tobacco barn hoping the sunshine blonde, Jillian, wasn't stalling progress. Pulling the zipper of her coat up, Sam groaned inwardly before putting on a smile.

"Morning, Jake. Thanks for coming so quick. It's the darnedest thing. Quinn said not a one of them ran long and the older Honda four-wheeler didn't even try to start." Jake Foster wasn't just the only local mechanic but also one of the few people in Milford who really knew how terrifying the night was when Becky disappeared . They spoke on occasion, usually when Sam needed his mechanical talents, but never spoke of that night. Anytime Sam found herself in his company, a flood of memories followed and she sensed he felt the same way.

Jake was bad boy handsome, with his shaggy dark hair and low hip jeans, and Jillian Crest appeared just as smitten with greasy hands and light eyes as she had been for bearded dark eyed game wardens. Apparently if it was male and had a heartbeat, she was swooned.

"He looks capable enough to figure it out," Jillian purred causing the corners of Jake's wide mouth to lift in the corners. This one could give Felicity Brown a run for her money, Sam mused.

Jake pulled on a rubbery line, spewing gas everywhere. If he only knew how much that set Sam back he wouldn't be so wasteful. Sam bit the inside of her cheek. This was going to be costly.

"Well there's your problem." Both women hovered above him, trying to see what he saw. Sam knew how to handle emergencies, she'd raised a child alone, but her knowledge of anything with a motor is where she was the amateur.

"I don't see a problem. It's gas." No oil she could see. A little thick maybe? A cold nip of wind flung her hair into her face and one of Professor Porter's lessons came back to her. *Cold didn't freeze gasoline*, she silently murmured to herself.

"Sugar," Jake solved that mystery. "You have sugar in the gas tanks." Sam reeled back and blinked.

"How did sugar get in a gas tank?" Jillian asked making a pip sound as if she thought he was kidding. He wasn't.

"All of them?" Sam asked.

"I'll know in a minute, but my guess is, yeah." Jake stood, brushed off his jeans and moved to the Honda four-wheeler next. Same result. That didn't make sense.

"How," Sam muttered questionably.

"My guess, someone put it there." Jake was commonly a sarcastic wit, but Sam could see even he was confused by the diagnosis. "I can fix it, but," he paused, shuffling his feet. "Excuse us will you," he addressed Jillian. To Sam's surprise she did just that, a pout following her back towards the lodge.

"Sam, you should call the sheriff." He pierced her with a serious worried look.

"The sheriff? You think kids did this?" No one had ever done anything like this before. Surely there was some other explanation.

"Intentional act or bad prank, either way Ron should know." Her head was spinning, trying to make sense out of why someone would purposely do such a thing. Did they not see how much something like this would cost her, and during her peak season at that?

"Can you clean the tanks so I can have them running by this evening? My clients won't take kindly to walking out of there in the dark tonight." She asked hopeful.

"Well, I could have simply cleaned them but they started them. The nine hundred Ranger even made it out to the driveway. Sorry to say but that means I need to flush the lines, replace fuel filters, and maybe the fuel injectors too." Jake pocketed his hands letting her absorb the news. "I'll have to order everything. No one near carries supplies for off road vehicles around here." This day was getting better and better.

"Fine," she huffed, slapping a heavy arm against her side. "Do what you need to." They stood there for a moment. Sam trying to estimate the cost, Jake trying to ask questions he didn't feel proper asking. She sat aside thinking someone had destroyed personal property and focused on him instead. That was easier to conquer right now.

With the fresh discovery that Becky had been found, Jake had to be going through the same plaguing regrets she had all these years. "You should go see her." Sam said cautiously.

"Who?" Jake followed her gaze towards the house. Sam knew he was itching to ask how Nelly was. Underneath what wore on him now, Jake had always been close with Nell. The downtrodden clung to her graces and warm meals.

"Not sure I should cause her more hurt. Nelly was always good to me, back then you know." Sam hadn't known all about Jake's childhood just bits and pieces and it seemed Nelly's fairness to treat everyone as equals meant something different to him than in her own personal experience.

"You didn't hurt her," Sam said sternly.

"The newspaper said she was the second identified. The sheriff came to see me too. I think I'm even a suspect." He ran his fingers through his hair, letting out a heavy sigh before his pinned-up thoughts released. "My lands Sam, to think she was here, right under us all these years."

"I know. It's hard to accept sometimes. I'm sorry you are going through this again. I'm sorry for all of us," Sam began.

"But for her the most," he said pointing a thumb towards the lodge. "Becky loved her momma." Jake nodded his head. "Wanted to be just like her she did. I think she even wanted to adopt children someday. We quarreled over it once. What fourteen-year-old boy wanted to talk about babies?" His last words were mumbled but Sam heard them clearly. Jake wasn't all spit and vinegar. He was a man broken from a childhood that followed him into all the next stages of his life. An abusive father, a negligent mother, and life single and alone without someone to share your thoughts with, and worst of all, watching the one person who made your life better be taken while screaming out your name. Guilt was passed out evenly between them it seemed.

"You should go in. It would be good for her and I think for you too," Sam urged and to her surprise, Jake Foster followed her into the house he hadn't stepped into in almost twenty-years.

Sam did a little work on her website until she heard Jake leave. She found Nelly in the kitchen pulling a pan of fresh muffins from the oven. Baking always soothed her. Her favorite apron, a polka dotted green faded treasure, draped over a blue button up shirt and jeans. It was a common scene that warmed her and was proof that talking with Jake had done her good.

"Those clients of yours sure have an appetite," Nelly smiled. She was in her element here, in the kitchen, feeding the world. Sam smiled back. Her life had been routine, and now it was a roller coaster of twist and turns. She still hadn't deciphered Quinn's almost kiss or Brody's private hope for a family. Now they were all reliving a hurt they had worked hard to soothe. Her mountain had changed everything and was now the most popular place on the map, but for all the wrong reasons.

"Where did Jillian and the others go? I saw them climb into Whitley's Chevy."

"Shopping," Nelly huffed. "Those women haven't stopped talking about shopping so I gave them directions." Nelly was no fan of shopping or rooms full of women.

"I hate going to the grocery store," Sam admitted with a grin.

"What's wearing on your thoughts?" Nelly popped in a second tray, this time blueberry muffins.

"Just a lot to absorb," Sam replied.

"I imagine so. We have been handed our share of troubles, have we not child?" It went without saying.

"Life has a way of knocking you down, doesn't it?" Sam poured herself a cup of coffee and added the perfect amount of creamer. Taking a sip, she began placing the cooled applesauce muffins in a plastic container.

"I'm fifty-eight and still understand nothing. Sit down, tell an old woman your thoughts. Mine are probably not as interesting." Sam would have laughed if not for her current thoughts being so overwhelming.

"I'm glad you talked with Jake. I think he needed that."

"We both did. He's still a good boy. I hate he is being drug back into all of this. Not a soul in this county believed him capable of hurting my Becky. I know he cared for her and sometimes I dream of her on her wedding day." Nelly folded the hand towel and smoothed it out as her thoughts drifted.

"It's Jake I see her walking down the aisle with too." She shook her head. "Jake will be fine, he was born to handle burdens and shoulder hurts. Now what else is troubling that mind of yours? Think I have forgotten you have a birthday coming or something?" Nelly spoke as only a mother-in-law could do to a thirty-two-year-old woman. Her upcoming birthday was furthest from her thoughts.

"There's the matter of the gas tanks. Jake thinks I should tell the sheriff. That it was deliberate."

"Then we shall call him," Nelly replied matter a fact.

Sam let out a weary sigh. "It just seems God takes a lot. Which is a cruel thing to say to you, I know. But some days it feels like you can never get ahead of the losses."

"God didn't do any of this mess. Man did. Men always make a muck of things."

"Do you believe in fate Nelly? I mean, that we are simply meant to meander through life, simply do our best and only hope it's enough?"

"I believe in God. I also believe it's time for you to start facing what's in front of you." Nelly sat and brought her cup to her thin lips and sipped.

"Could you narrow that down? Currently there is a lot going on in front of me." Nelly chuckled.

"God's plan is not for you to be alone forever." Nelly lifted a sharp thin brow.

"I have Brody, you, and this place. I'm not lonely." Sam smarted and gripped at her cup feeling bruised.

"You're not as smart as you look sometimes," Nelly wobbled her head. "Look at things my way, the right way," Nelly winked. "Me and Clayton married and wanted a family. So we built a house with the faith that God would help us fill it."

"Wants and wishes are a waste. How many times have you preached that? You had that and it is all gone. You can't say that doesn't make you angry with Him."

"I can, and will say it. He gave me exactly what I asked for, and more. He supplied my needs, gave me healthy babies, and a man who loved me until he took his last breath." Sam admired her optimism but one could not see beauty in so much loss, could they?

"I lost them, yes, but it was better than not having them at all." Sam hadn't thought about it that way. "Did you know when my Dale was young he was such a handful. Always getting into things, testing my patience?"

"I can see that," Sam grinned though she knew all too well how Dale Quinn could test a woman's patience.

"Then, Clayton's brother Howard and his wife were killed all of a sudden in that car crash and little Henry was brought to our doorstep." Nelly stared across the table, smiled at the memory.

"I've heard the story."

"Well this is the parts you don't know. Clayton welcomed Henry with open arms. He was so happy to have his brother's son under his roof, another boy to add to the fold. Me on the other hand," Nelly sat back. "I was pregnant with Aaron, exhausted with Dale, and as horrible as it sounds, I was scared to death of this little brown eyed boy and having even more responsibility laid on me. I even prayed God find him a family. That someone would come take him so I wouldn't have to be his momma too." Sam remained silent in that confession. It didn't sound like the woman she had known at all.

"I couldn't see myself taking on another child. I was overwhelmed already and thought it was unfair I was asked to raise a child, not my own. I wasn't always a kind-hearted woman." Sam had never known Nelly ever felt that way.

"But Henry was smart, even at that age." Nelly wagged a finger. "He knew my heart even if I didn't say it out loud. But like you've done all these years, I took the hand dealt me and sucked it up. I kept my fear and worries to myself and did what was expected of me. Keep on keeping on, you know?" Sam knew, she had watched and learned such from her. Nelly's heart was pure gold under all that country lady bossiness.

"Our Henry was so young, heartbroken, and now living with mere strangers that he knew might not love him." Sam felt her heart break, hearing this side of the story. "He cried for a few days for his momma, but then one day when Aaron started teething and Dale had just the day before broken his arm, and I was ready to pull all my hair out, Henry just stopped. Like he knew this was how life was supposed to be now, that he needed to stand back and only take what was given him." That sounded like the man she was discovering too.

"I saw to his needs, but I didn't hold him. He lost his momma and she was replaced by a home full of screaming babies with a deranged woman at the helm," Nelly chuckled. "My Henry has always been that way, seeing those around him fared better than him. It's one of his most admirable qualities."

Nelly beamed, talking about a younger Quinn. The house was filled with dozens of pictures of Henry as a boy. Like Brody he was adorable and cute, but those bulging brown eyes of Quinn's always held hollowness, one that darkened into blackness with time.

"Well, anyways, one day I was feeding Aaron in one room, while in another Dale was playing with a candle. By the time I smelled the singe of carpet, Henry had it put out and took the blame too. I knew better and hugged him for it. I looked at that little boy willing to take a whooping for something Dale did and was proud that he was now my son too. It was just that simple thing. Not only did he keep the house from burning down and Dale from hurting himself, but he defended Dale when he didn't deserve it. That day Dale changed too." She waved a finger. "He no longer wanted to destroy and make noise for no reason. He wanted to be like Henry."

Sam swallowed hard. She could see it now. Dale had always looked up to him, admired Quinn's accomplishments.

"Dale looked up to him like Henry was the elder brother and soon Henry was that to all my children. I think Aaron wanted to be a soldier because Henry always talked about protecting people. You should have seen Henry's face when he held Becky the first time,"

Nelly's voice cracked. A tear drifted slowly down her cheek. Sam remained silent, nursing her own tears. Nelly needed this time to talk freely.

"He thanked me for giving him a baby sister. I cried like a baby, Clayton too though he never would admit it. Her birth made us all a family Clayton said. No more nephew, aunt, or uncle." Nelly leaned forward. "I say, we became a family when Henry walked into that door."

"I never knew that," Sam replied. She found that even though she was still at odds with the man, the boy was worthy of admiration.

"When all that death came to me, Henry was there for me in return. Everything I lost, the hurt I felt, we shared it. I went through the angry parts like most," Nelly chaffed. "God took my husband, my sons, and my daughter, but you know what?"

"You still had Henry," Sam answered.

"Yes. I still had my boy. He found me crying in the dirt of my flower bed after we got word about Aaron. He knelt down there with me and said, "Aunt Nelly, it will always hurt, but God won't take that which He cannot fill again. I would have never survived losing the rest of them if not for that."

"I don't understand," Sam puzzled at the logic.

"I have Brody, my grandson. I have Henry, and I have you. My house and my heart have never been empty. I have never been without someone to love. You're lonely, because you won't look at what's around you. You won't let yourself see what everyone else sees." With that Nelly wiped her apron over her damp face and went back to baking without another word.

Connie arrived while Sam was folding laundry and pondering over Nelly's words. Connie absent-mindedly started folding, a womanly instinct perhaps. Her long dangling earrings bounced and glittered gold as she laughed catching Sam up on the latest gossip. Connie was a true friend, but at times she butted in and forced Sam to deal. No wonder her kids got into Ivy League colleges with that tenaciousness. Perhaps Sam was her own worst enemy, and though she would never admit it, she was lonely.

"Okay, time to spill it. I don't want to talk on my day off about Mrs. Jennings pitching a fit because Felicity turned her hair purple or how much money you saved on a turkey yesterday. We shop the same grocery store." Connie smarted as she sat on the old brown sofa and lifted a muffin to her mouth. "I can see your mind is working overtime and it has nothing to do with sugared gas tanks or what's going on up on that mountain." Connie added and bit into a second muffin. "This is going to ruin my diet," she moaned and took another bite, making the whole thing disappear. Sam sat in the leather chair across from her, glad they were alone.

"He doesn't need to be here. He should leave." Sam finally admitted.

"I knew it." Connie slapped her thigh. "It's about time we can talk about this." Sam flinched.

"You're so dramatic." Sam chuckled then let out a weary sigh. "It's weird having him here all the time," Sam said picking at her nails nervously. She needed to talk to someone about what was troubling her, keeping her awake at night.

"I bet," Connie grinned, reaching for another muffin.

"He tucks Brody into bed every night. That's my job, and it's a little nerve racking that someone can waltz in here and simply take over, fit in, and nobody notices a thing."

"Stop kicking against the man like an ill-tempered mule. It's ugly to watch. Brody needs a man in his life, you said so yourself."

"I still feel that way, but…" Sam didn't know how to explain to her closest and dearest friend she was having feelings, feelings about a man who wasn't worth her time, a man that had a reputation.

"But now you're seeing things differently?" Connie looked her square in the eye.

"Perhaps I am. I've been alone along time. His presence is throwing me off. It was different when he came here while I was working. Now we sat at the same table." Sam leaned forward, lowering her voice. "We share the same bathroom. His toothbrush sits next to ours."

Connie laughed, causing Sam to bristle. "Don't know many women in this town who would sympathize with ya." Connie waved an arm in the air. "Share a meal with a handsome man, every night. Have a son who adores him, and oh, I get it. He leaves the seat up. He's flawed and I now see what all the fuss is." Sam didn't find it funny at all.

"You don't get it," Sam huffed, crossing both arms over her chest.

"Oh, I get it. You can't admit you have feelings for the handsome, rugged, chivalrous, game warden." Sam's eyes went wide, stirring another laugh out of her friend.

"Dale thought of him as a brother. They were raised in the same house, by the same woman. Nelly admitted just today she claims him as a son. It's…weird." Sam got to her feet and started to pace nervously. It was hard to look dignified and poised with such heavy thoughts. "I should not be thinking the thoughts I'm thinking, I need to get my head checked."

"I know a guy that can do wonders with muddled brains," Connie said teasingly. "And for the record, they aren't brothers. Now if he was *your* brother…" Her teasing had no end.

"He's a good one, Sam. He doesn't step on toes, cross lines, and doesn't look bad in uniform. What more could a woman ever want than to be loved by a man like that?"

"Love? That's foolishness. No one said anything about love," Sam flapped a hand in the air. "And if he knew me so well, then why has he ignored me all these years, barely looking me in the eye when I could have used a shoulder to cry on? Where was he before I fell in a pit of bodies?" She couldn't stop when the tears came. They had a mind of their own these days. Connie got to her feet and held her.

"Waiting," Connie said in a grave voice. "He did try Sam, in the best way he knew how. What's important is Henry has never wandered far. He has always been near, watching over you." Sam wasn't sure that was true. "It wasn't our place to say anything. That is his job." She released her hold but kept a hand on Sam's shoulder. "He's the one who told me to hire you. Begged me actually," Connie confessed.

"He did?" Why had no one ever told her these things before?

"He comes by on your days off to check the schedule. Oh, he pretends its social, and Monty, Cindy, and I get our kicks over it. Fact is, he stays in the shadows but keeps close tabs. Why else would he have gotten so upset I had you put in a dress and took you to the Brick with us?"

"I knew you did that on purpose," Sam scolded.

"And though you don't like to talk about it, I'll say this and no more because with everything going on, I know you're about wrung out." Sam doubted this was the end of what Connie had to say but let her continue. "He and Dale have gone to blows plenty... over you."

"Why would you keep this kind of thing from me?" Betrayal stung as sharp as a lie.

"You wouldn't have listened. Not then. You were so caught up in all the things against you that you didn't want to listen to anything that could be good for you." Had she? "You had this idea of who Henry was because Dale told you things. Didn't you ever wonder why, when Dale thought him the best man he ever knew, his brother, he would say such mean things about him?"

"I thought he was just warning me like overprotective husbands do." It sounded ridiculous now that she admitted so out loud. Images of years of quick glances and distance trespassed into her thoughts.

"Exactly." That word held new meaning and Sam swallowed it for the hard lump it was.

"I don't know what to say." And she didn't.

Bones on the Mountain

CHAPTER SIXTEEN

Some obsessions kill.

Quinn paced the floor in the sitting room, waiting for the sheriff to arrive. Ron said he had news. He also said seven thirty and he was late. Nelly let Brody help scoop ice cream for the clients to keep them all in the kitchen, bragging about the day's hunt over peach cobbler. James Crest had successfully taken down Zeus and Quinn's muscles were still stiff as frozen logs after dragging the massive deer back to the truck. He was cold, angry, and now knowing why his morning started off with everything going wrong, he had another reason to get his own hands on the culprits that sugared the utility vehicle's gas tanks.

Sam sat on the sofa, a picture of patience. Her jeans bore a small tear at the knee. Her blue pullover sweater, a green and button up, made her eyes deeper today.

Quinn stopped pacing, let out an agitated breath, and focused on the woman. A man struggled to stay mad for long with her near.

She was air and light and a sack full of tomorrows. If only she knew how much he loved her, how far he would go, for her.

Head down, brows gathered, she was likely counting the cost she refused to tell him that Jake would require to fix the vehicles. He would gladly pay the cost, but he knew that would be shot down so he kept quiet. At some point he would have to come clean, tell her everything, but today wasn't that day. Knowing someone snuck around outside without him aware, pitted his gut. How could he prove himself worthy of protecting her and Brody after someone so easily crept past his defenses?

Sensing his eyes on her, Sam picked up one of three magazines on the coffee table, glanced at the pages, but he knew she wasn't reading a single word. He found a seat next to her and leaned back, waiting. Apparently sheriffs didn't abide by the same tardiness rules they handed out to their deputies.

He gave Sam a sideways glance. She'd braided her hair and a few strands had found their way out of the twisted tangle. He was tempted to touch them, tucked them in securely. The hardwood floor had two large fur rugs and currently her bare feet were snuggling into one of them.

"Are you worried," he asked lowly.

"Why would I be?" She wrinkled her nose. "Jake just thinks it was kids playing a prank. Still, Ron should tend to it so it doesn't happen again," she spoke coolly, but he knew she wondered who would do such a thing.

"I was thinking," Quinn started.

"Don't." She faced him. "This is not your problem Quinn and I can handle this just as I handle emergencies every day." Her delicate chin lifted stubbornly.

"I agree, but I already called the service." He glared back.

"Service?"

"I'm having security cameras installed, around the house, the barn, and the drive. They'll be here in an hour to get it done." She stared at him, speechless. He was overstepping in her eyes, but she'd just have to accept it.

"No more surprises," That was his hope.

"And yet, they just keep coming," she rolled her eyes stubbornly. "You want to help cook dinner so Nelly can have a night off. Preferably the same night Ron gets off," she said with a knowing brow. Quinn's forehead creased. Had he missed something else? He gave his head a mental slap for ignorance.

"I grill. I don't cook. In fact, I burn even the thought of cooking. Trust me, you don't want me to do that," he smirked.

"How have you not starved," she gave him a casual look over. "Never mind, I already know." She turned back to her magazine. He knew what she was thinking. What she always thought. God only knew what things Dale whispered into her ear.

Dale had always liked what others had...or what they wanted. He knew Quinn crushed over Sam, yet Dale pursued her in his absence. Then Nelly called about the wedding and Quinn had no choice but let go of the hope he would come back to Milford and find her waiting for him. So he stayed gone, refused visits and took his first job far from Milford.

In his first year as a wildlife officer down south he dated Melody, a sweet preacher's daughter who had no interest in anything to do with the outdoors. After three months Quinn found her once attractive cleanliness more of a mental issue. When he bought the house in Lewis there was Jules. Her fast pace intrigued him as much as her flashy smile. She liked everything he did, right down to the Bengals who were becoming an embarrassment that year. Off and on they played the part of a couple between jobs, but in the end Jules wanted more and Quinn couldn't commit. Sitting beside him now, he knew why. A few dates after he turned thirty and Quinn still found nothing compared to the shadow of the woman who stole his heart all those years ago.

It was her and she was everywhere. Her laugh danced on windy spring days, her essence wafted over him every time he walked outdoors, breathed fresh air, and he needed her as much as he needed to breathe. It was her he hoped to cross paths with in every bakery and coffee shop he entered. Her he wanted in the passenger seat as he logged miles on the roadways. And she thought him a scoundrel.

"Your impression of me is starting to border rudeness." He said in a graveled tone.

"It's not an impression. Dale spoke often of your many...cooks." Sam got to her feet as she always did after a rude remark, making a quick exit. Today, Quinn was in no mood to let her run off after one. He stood and moved faster, stepping in her path.

"And I would appreciate you stop bargaining with my son," she snapped. She didn't like confrontation, any more than she liked changing her mindset apparently.

"That's enough." He hadn't meant to raise his voice, not to her, but he had never stepped on shade on her side of the fence. What did he have to do to make her see him and not some made up version of him?

"Excuse me." She tried on a fierce defiance. Those stormy eyes met his and it was all he could do not to crush his lips on hers right then. Smother her doubts, show his intentions, and leave her knowing she had been thoroughly kissed by a man who had waited a long time to deliver it.

"I thought you were smarter than that Samantha." Those dark onyx eyes steeled her more than his maven tone. "How can you be so naive to believe I could ever be anything other than who I am?"

Her attention was caught and she tried looking away, ignoring the man, but her heart was leading while her head spun wildly. She hated being wrong as much as being lied to and there were no doubts left. His eyes burned, narrowed, and then landed on her lips. This was not the position Sam wanted to be in again.

"What do you want from me, Quinn?" Her voice was demanding but inside, Sam was awakening, the intensity quivering her every cell. She prided herself on being stronger, but she knew she was outmatched.

"Look at me Sam," he demanded, pushing past walls she had so masterfully constructed. Years alone didn't shroud the look of a man with intent. She'd remembered such sensations, such longing, but never to a point of being unquenchable.

Quinn lowered his head, but his eyes remained open and locked firmly onto to hers. For a brief second Sam considered throwing caution to the wind, grab hold and let herself fall. He was just a breath away.

Coming to her senses she placed a hand on his chest and pushed back. "Henry," she said in a hushed breath. "We can't. It's…"

"Long over due." He stepped closer. "I reckon I measured a hundred reasons why not to kiss you, until now." She didn't' have a second to react before his lips were on hers. Warm and reckless, and like the brute that he was.

Then she fell.

The kiss was absolute mastery, a combination between hunger and diversion. The scent of his skin, the slide of his hands tipping her head, urging her lips to open to him, all sent waves of euphoria over her. His thumb settled on the leaping pulse of her neck. That simple touch caused a hot rush through her entire body. Sam wrapped both hands around his neck to keep her trembling knees from buckling. He swallowed every last resistance she had left.

If they didn't need air to live, Sam could have stayed right there for a while. Forehead to forehead, breath to breath, they remained connected. The wild rhythm in his chest, pounding under her hand.

"I tried not to want you. I tried all this time, but…"

Sam blinked in the shock of his words. "I don't know how to respond to that," she removed her hand from him and placed it on her own chest. "To this," she stammered.

"Take a minute then," he grinned devilishly. "Lord knows I spent years on it myself. But know this, it's time to stop building walls up between us Sam. I'm done walking around them." No, Henry Quinn walked through them. Dreams were lousy substitutes for the real thing.

"Why me?"

"Who else could there ever be," he said with such conviction she wanted to believe him.

The clearing of a throat stopped the moment cold. Sam was thankful Ron finally showed up and quickly stepped away from Quinn. He didn't seem at all bothered or embarrassed to be caught in each other's arms. In fact, Quinn seemed put out with Ron for disrupting them.

"Sorry to interrupt," Ron grinned and stepped into the room. "I came as soon as I could get free. Those federal agents are more needy than a one-legged dog." He removed his hat. "You seem to be healing rather nicely."

"I have good genes," Sam jested, hoping the local sheriff hadn't been standing in the doorway long. Her eyes went from Ron to Quinn, both looking at her amused.

"So with this business with your four-wheelers, Jake gave me his thoughts so I need to ask..." Ron paused. "Could Brody have done it?"

"Brody isn't that kind of kid. Adventurous maybe, but he wouldn't even toy with such an idea." Quinn said sternly. She appreciated Quinn defending her son in as much as he knew Brody incapable of doing such a thing.

"Sheriff, I'm sure it was just teenagers being teenagers, and I know you have your plates full and stacked up right now, but I can't afford another prank." Sam said firmly.

"Truth is unless some kid brags to a friend of a friend, I can't know. I had my deputies' dust for prints, but not sure it will turn up anything but Jake's greasy fingers now." Ron said.

"Sam," Ron motioned towards the couch. "Can we sit and talk about other things for a moment." Not words she wanted to hear right now with lips still tingling from Quinn's kiss.

"Sheriff, I have told you everything I remember as a child and about that day I fell." Sam said.

"Let's hear him out Sam. There has been a lot about the investigation I wanted to share with you before now." Quinn added and she shot him a puzzled glance.

"Then why haven't you?"

"It's kind of hard to get you to listen to a word I say," he said flatly. Well, she couldn't argue him that. "But now that I know how to quiet you," he smirked, "I'll be more forthcoming in the future."

If someone checked her temperature right now, she'd nearly die of embarrassment. Quietly, she sat back down, folded her hands together on her lap, and hoped no more would be mentioned.

The sheriff, disinterested, sat and leaned forward. With both elbows on his knees, he rolled the brim of his hat between hands.

"I guess you know by now we have at least identified sixteen women," Ron started.

"No, I didn't know that. The paper said nine." 16. Her bones chilled instantly at the idea that so many had died on her mountain. "I thought that was...." She clutched her hands together tighter for focus and spoke as calmly as if sitting behind the nerve center desk. "So this person murdered sixteen women on our mountain." It wasn't a question, more a fact to tell herself. "Have you told Nelly this?"

"Nelly knows. I've kept her in the loop the best I can without stepping out of line." Ron admitted. "There are more to be identified."

"More!" *More than sixteen.* Sam was sure they were all living out the newest whodunit with three more books to go.

"Not sure they will even all be identified," Ron added not holding back. "We have missing person's reports that seem to help form a pattern, and have an idea on a dozen or so, but nothing concrete yet. DNA works fast but we aren't there yet." Poor Ron, Sam sympathized. For as hard as this was to learn, it was him who was having to tell sixteen mother's that their children had been found.

"Where do they think he came from?" She said in a low voice. Perhaps focusing on the details would be easier than imagining so many young Becky's buried together.

"Not far. No more than a hundred miles or so away." Quinn put in. *So he could be a local,* she thought. Yes, details made it easier to think and not imagine herself into a public display of tears.

Focus Sam.

"Profiler has him as a local. No more than a town over maybe. A white male, between the age of twenty-five and fifty-five," Ron looked to Quinn, who nodded before he continued. "They think him someone who works steady in a trade or profession, and has few friends, and none-to-little family. Single, though most serial killers have relationships, a ruse to hide themselves. He lives simply, few possessions, and possibly OCD."

"A profiler can tell all of that by a few bones and pictures?" Sam cocked her head to him.

"It's their job to know. This guy Morrow is good they tell me. He's worked on cases like this, well, similar to this, before." Ron said. "Sam, he didn't kill her or any of those women here."

"But we found them." Quinn reached over and gripped her hand, indicating Ron was only warming up. Sam steadied herself for the next torrent wave.

"He takes them somewhere else, a home or building maybe," he ran his hand over his bald head.

"How does he do it?" She clenched her jaw. "What does he do to them?"

"No!" Quinn said sharply.

"I can't share that information and I wouldn't even if I could." Ron said frankly. Did she really want the sordid details of Becky's last moments to accompany her current nightmares?

"I don't know what all you remember about the night you spent down there, but could you try to describe it to me again?"

"Not much. It was dark, and cold. I kept fading in and out of consciousness," she started and felt her hand being squeezed slightly. Just reliving that night brought a chill over her, but Quinn looked just as he had that night. Worried, concerned. No one ever worried over her like that before.

"I remember holding the bone I found and trying to get up. I couldn't. Everything hurt, even my eye lids. The floors were hard and littered with acorn hulls or something, but I drifted off again until I heard Quinn call to me." She kept that scary imagine she thought she imagined, to herself.

"Not acorns," Ron mumbled.

"Those were beetles castings, mostly dead." Quinn added. For the next twenty minutes Sam learned all about the Dermestid Beetle from their need for dark places to their gruesome capabilities. No one needed to paint the picture of what the sheriff was implying and her stomach twisted at the gruesome facts. Quinn was right. Sam didn't want to know anymore.

"One more question. I know this is a lot, but one of the folks up there helping out found a camera."

"One of the deer cams, yes. I have them all over the mountain." So now she was three side by sides, one four-wheeler, and one camera short.

"All over the mountain?" Quinn said shooting Ron a look.

"Sam, exactly how many of those cameras do you have scattered across those hills?" Ron asked.

"Nineteen now, but sometimes less. On occasion batteries die or locals find them and turn them off so I can't see them wandering off the path to the park." Sam sat up straighter.

"Does that happen often? The turning off thing, I mean?" Quinn asked. Sam hesitated in answering. The sheriff and the warden were fishing, at what, she wasn't sure.

"Not really and its usually the Moore's hopping over the hill hoping I don't see them stealing ginseng in August."

"Ever get pictures of two legged animals?" Ron quickly inquired. She didn't know who to answer first.

"A few over the years," she told the sheriff. "We're connected to the park so a lot of locals on ATV's or horseback use the ridge line to travel. We never minded before. Everyone knows during hunting season it isn't safe and abide by it well enough. I hang signs too."

"Like who all? I want a list." Ron switched to his more professional tone.

"Heck sheriff. Half the town," Sam's voice pitched. "Do you really think someone who would kill then construct such a place, use nature and flesh-eating bug to hide his crimes, would be dumb enough to be caught on camera?"

"We can hope," Ron said getting to his feet. Sam took a breath. Was it possible one of the many faces she had deleted from memory cards over the years could hold the identity of a killer?

"We will narrow it down and get you a list by morning," Quinn said as the sheriff replaced his hat and gave a satisfied nod.

"Sorry about all of this Sam and we will take the vandalism serious, but understand we are running shorthanded right now."

"I'm sorry too. Sorry for all of us."

"We all have a stake in this one." That was true. Becky was loved by many, not just Sam or her family, and there were others. Families who lost their daughters who needed to know justice would be served. "Oh, one more thing," Ron hesitated before stepping out of the room. "The clothes you wore that day, where are they?"

"Nelly tossed them in the trash. Why?"

"No reason, just curious is all. Good day to ya both. I'm going to speak with Nelly for a moment and get back to the office."

CHAPTER SEVENTEEN

Sam jolted at the sound of the radiator in the far corner then chided herself for letting something so familiar frighten her. Against Quinn's wants, she had returned to work. It was that or go crazy at home knowing she had walked that hill a hundred times a year and missed Becky being there all this time.

She didn't miss the scents of musky cold concrete and unnatural hours, but it was better being a lifeline to folks than needing one. Here she was practiced, in her comforts of knowing what to do next. At home, Sam was treading water and getting tired. Her heart was being lost and her head simply wasn't taking over to keep her above water.

Now she understood how her own father put all his energies into work. For the last three days she tried to slip back into routine, a sense of normalcy, but with more outside interest filling the small town, things were still far from normal.

She had dodged a very persistent young man from a news station Friday when dropping Brody off at school. It came as no surprise she had to dodge him a second time by sneaking out of the back of the local clinic after having her stitches removed. There was a killer out there, and now the whole world knew it. Another thing about small towns, everyone knew everything about each other.

Thanks to her dad and Quinn, Brody had taken a liking to games, so evenings passed with a series of Chutes and Ladders and Ants in the Pants. Sam got the full report each morning. It was good her son appeared unaffected. Children need not worry over killers and graves and real monsters.

Quinn had become more cautious, protective in a way she had never known before. He always held that air, but Sam wasn't accustomed to being the center of it. Now he insisted on driving Brody to school each morning before spending his days helping track down a killer. Sam let out a long sigh. What was she going to do with him? The man even made her coffee this morning and surprisingly, Sam didn't have to tell him how she liked it.

"When a man knows how you take your coffee, he pays attention," Connie had said with one of her common I-told-ya-so smirks. Only it wasn't Connie's heart being lost now was it?

Since that kiss, Sam had done a lot of thinking. A woman who lost over and over was a fool to purposefully set herself up for another. She would be a fool not to admit to how she truly felt. How her feelings had blossomed into something she so desperately wanted to explore. She felt the same attraction, the same warm giddiness she had as a teen. How many hours had she watched a younger Henry Quinn catch, bat, and outrun the opponents, stopping them from taking the win? How many hearts had she secretly squiggled on notebooks while waiting for puberty to endow her willowy frame?

She was no longer a girl, and he was no longer a boy. They were two quiet people, holding on as best they could to the hand dealt them. They both knew loss, heartache. He said he cared for her, had always cared. Those words hadn't escaped her. He'd honored her marriage to Dale, despite knowing Dale had not.

She was drawn to him, intrigued by him, and angry with herself for thinking him no better than the man she fool-heartedly gave her heart to. He protected everything around him, including her and her son. And she believed he truly loved her. He hadn't said the words, and she was no regular to romances, but it was in his eyes and gentle movements. It was in the way his eyes smiled when she stepped into a room, and the way his hands went into his pockets anytime she drew near. Such control after only days ago, ravishing her with lips and angst.

Footfalls on the stairs quickly revealed Kate Carmichael coming on to her shift. Sam got to her feet, pushed aside any further thinking of the local warden who was probably sitting outside right now waiting to drive her home.

"Morning Sam," Kate's always perky voice greeted. "Have an easy night?" Kate was doing wonderful with her training, Connie mentioned. Her North Face down parka hugged her healthy torso.

Kate was a beautiful girl and Sam suspected she was the reason for deputy Alex Cane to meander downstairs so often. Sam retrieved her own coat and handed over the helm.

"Not much," Sam said sliding into her green jacket. She never liked the bulk of a heavy coat but was a good fan of layers. Country living was all about the thermal underwear and wool socks in winter and Sam had plenty of both.

"Kelly Simpson reported a possible break in at the flower shop but Clark thinks a coon or something had set off her alarms. We had a couple 23-01's down at the Brick. Darlene had the Everett Brother's sitting at a table with their heads hung in shame by the time Ron got there." Sam laughed. The Everett brothers were seeing the judge first thing Monday morning and looking at possibly serving a couple years for their poaching crimes already. Quinn would be glad that after last night, chances were they would be locked up for a while.

"23-01? That's public intoxication, right?" Kate asked hopeful.

"You're learning. Just keep going over the cheat sheet. I promise it will take no time to learn each code. Who's training with you today?" Sam wished she was, but she had to all but beg Connie as it was to return to work with all that was going on. Sam seldom played the single mom card but had no troubling whipping it out was it necessary.

"That would be Cindy. She is pretty wonderful to work with, but she texted me she would be five minutes late. No worries." Sam wasn't worried. If Cindy said five minutes, then it would be three.

"Oh and I noticed you brought a peanut butter sheet cake yesterday for the guys upstairs," Sam casually mentioned.

"I like to bake," Kate said bashfully, her cheeks flushing immediately.

"Just a heads up, our nice-looking young deputy, is allergic to peanuts but I hear he is a regular to Miller's Bakery. Something about cinnamon rolls and apple turnovers." Sam shot her a wink.

"Thank you Sam." Kate said grinning ear to ear. Yep, the new deputy would be drowning in sugary treats all winter. "Any more word on...you know," Kate shrugged. Quinn had been faithful keeping Sam informed. The FBI interviewed many locals, including a taxidermist, two men who drove trucks for a living, and Jake Foster. It barbed her to think he was enduring the same treatments all over. If Jake had any part in Becky's disappearance, she would have seen it that night. No, what she saw was a frantic young man, helpless to stop Becky from being taken from him.

"None. Have a good day Kate."

Outside the wind had been set loose as if nature herself flipped a fan on high and laid down for a nap. Sam tugged the zipper of her coat as high as it would go and buried her nose in the warmth stored there.

As promised, Quinn's truck sat just across the street, his head down and the light from his phone illuminating his face. Men aged so much better than women, no tricks nor treatments required. She climbed inside and fastened her belt. The truck smelled just like the man who owned it, earthy with a hint of pine and soap. He wasn't making any of this easier.

"Morning sunshine," he smiled then pulled out onto the road. The tips of his hair were still damp from a morning shower. He needed a good trim.

"Good night you mean," she said. "You should know those Everett brothers got a good lecture from Darlene last night and a cell this morning." He lifted a brow and his smile came slow and proudly. "I thought Roger would yell all night but thankfully Pete picked them up and transported them over to Mason. I can't say this little agreement with Mason to jail all prisoners disturbs me now." She laughed.

"Good." He turned left out of town. "Brought you something." Sam followed his gaze to the center console where two cups of coffee sat. "Vanilla cream?" she nodded and accepted the cup, a smile just under the surface. It was best not to encourage him, at least until everything was over. "Church doesn't start until ten. Maybe you can get a few winks before then."

"It's better to just stay up. I'm off tomorrow and spending time with Brody comes before rest," she said and took a sip.

"Just Brody?" His eyes remained on the road. When she said nothing Quinn added. "I was thinking with everything going on here and school break coming up..." he paused. "I'd like to take you and Brody on a small trip."

"That's not a good idea," Sam said flatly and quickly turned her attention out the window. As much as a getaway would do them all good right now, more time with Quinn was not a going to happen.

"You haven't even asked where." The humor in his voice did nothing to sway her.

"It doesn't matter." She turned to face him. "I have work and you should probably be getting home. You could do a lot more to help with finding her killer if you weren't chauffeuring me and Brody around."

"Sam," Quinn said on a soft breath. "I can do both, but with someone out there, capable of doing what this monster has done and now all the vandalism, a getaway isn't such a bad idea."

"I think it is," she lifted her chin convincingly. His eyes narrow as they always did when they were at opposite sides of a matter.

"I want to be part of your lives." His voice grew serious.

"You always have been," she answered truthfully. "Always will be, in a way, I guess." It was truth, but not the answer he wanted to hear. He flipped the blinker and pulled off the road onto Highway 32. Sam wasn't surprised that he did. Of course at some point they would have to address this thing between them.

The Littleton's pasture looked crisp with crusted brittle blades. A few cows lingered near the fence, their breath forming clouds to mimic the cold blue morning sky. Quinn put the truck in park and sat there staring out the front windshield. He was working up to all the right words.

"Can we talk, openly?" She asked.

"Should there ever be another other way for us talk?"

"We both know Dale painted a picture of you. I know better now but I can't say that isn't still ingrained."

"He made mistakes, but he gave you Brody."

"He did," she lifted her chin at the mention of her son's name. "But he grew tired of me. I can't do that again."

"Samantha, I fell in love with you the moment you crossed that ball field. When we shook hands I thought…" He searched for the words.

"Me too," she locked eyes on him sending his pulse racing. "I used to come over to your family's house all the time hoping you would be visiting from school, catch a peek." She regretted being so honest and open now. But Sam was three feet in the water, might as well get wet.

"Dale told me stories of all your girlfriends and the wild parties you attended. When I turned sixteen I was baptized and part of it was getting over that crush."

"You crushed for me for four years?" He hiked the corner of his mouth in that knowledge.

"You apparently did that longer," she reminded him.

"I wish I knew. I thought you were happy and didn't want to interfere with that. And for the record, I never had girlfriends in college, nor did I go to parties. I worked full time, studied like crazy. And my friends, well most of them are wardens now too and one really good conservationist. He writes for magazines about the impacts of the world on the environment."

Oh the man was more perfect than she had imagined. How she wished she could trust love to be forever and true. "I wish I knew that. Seems we both trusted the wrong source. If I had known I would have waited for you to come home and flung myself at you."

"Hold on a minute." Quinn sat back and stared at her in wonder. He really could intimidate with those eyes.

"What are you doing?"

"Trying to picture Samantha Carver throwing herself at me," his grin was teasing but her pride was strong..

"What if I can't do this?"

"We," he turned to face her, "can do this."

"Brody looks up to you. This might confuse him, if you change your mind or find someone else." It was one thing to risk her heart, but not her son's too. He could have the fun Quinn, the stop by every so often Quinn. She could stop this now and no one would get hurt. Quinn reached for her cup and took it from her and set it back into the cup holder before taking her hand in his.

"You're reaching for straws darling. I'm more stubborn than you. I made up my mind long ago. If this is a trust issue…"

"It's not. I do trust you," she quickly put in.

"Then let me love you Samantha." Lifting her chin, Quinn leaned closer, stopping short of permission to proceed. Controlling these rolling emotions inside her already struggling resolve was wearing at her.

"Love isn't for everyone." Tears were right there, pooling and waiting for one blink to start them cascading into a water fall of bad decisions on the floor.

"Sam," his arms swallowed her whole. "I love you. I know you love me. Don't make me go another twenty years aching for you." Had he truly ached for her for twenty years? That wasn't possible.

"Love breaks your heart," she exploded. "It dies and tears and leaves. It's not there when you need it most. It's cruel and I can't bear having more of you and losing you. Love can do more damage to a heart than knowing there is always someone better, prettier," she cried.

"Oh baby," he said pulling her tighter to him. "That wasn't love. Love isn't one sided. Love bears all things, believes all things, hopes and endures all things." He kissed her damp cheek. "Love never fails." He kissed her forehead. "I don't remember the rest of the verse," he stared down at her.

"But love changes its mind." She wouldn't let him, years down the road, come to his senses and regret giving her his heart.

"How much more can a man prove his love to you? I have waited for you since you were twelve." He kissed her fingers. "You took an awful long time to grow up Samantha." He chuckled before leaning in to kiss her lips.

She suddenly forgot all the excuses, the reasons she couldn't love him and met him halfway. That meeting of hearts fulfilled a fresh hope, and there was passion reserved for them there. When they finally parted, Quinn held her face in both hands, brushing away tears with his thumbs.

"I haven't dated since I was seventeen. I might not be good at it," she said on a laugh.

Quinn growled and kissed her again. She had no idea how wonderful and perfect she was. But he would find a way to show her everyday how much he appreciated each second she was his, and he was starting right now.

"I'm not interested in dating," he said, leaning away from her.

"I don't understand." Even that look of bewilderment enhanced her beauty. Oh he loved this woman. He had planned it all out. The fine meal, the wine, but this was the perfect moment. Right here and right now with raw hearts and messy emotions.

"Do you love me Sam?" By the grace of God and a heart that was always hers, he sat beside her ready to make good every promise he hoped she would let him deliver.

"I do." She sobbed out.

"Good. Because I have loved you most of my life and I have never loved another." Quinn reached into the center console and removed the small box he'd been hording for years. Sam's hands crashed over her mouth as fresh tears ran down her flushed face. He opened the little velvety black box, watched her eyes go wide in shock at the diamonds encased in white gold he had so carefully chosen for this moment. Men weren't romantics, but she would never look more beautiful than this moment right here and he drank it in to store to memory forever.

"I don't want to date you, though I do think some date nights would be wonderful. And don't say this is too soon, when we have known each other, each flaw and hurt and accomplishment, most our lives. I don't want to leave. I want to stay, with you, for the rest of our lives. My heart has always been yours. All you have to do is trust me with yours." She wasn't looking at the ring that he had poured years and years of time into. She was looking at him, the man, all rugged and simple and trustworthy. It was a scary leap for her, he knew, but he also knew she was brave and capable and prayed she would simply trust him with her heart.

"Henry Quinn you were my first crush," her words said in tears. "How can I refuse you being my last? Yes." Quinn slipped the ring on her finger and kissed her with the promise of more.

CHAPTER EIGHTEEN

With eager hands he set the box down in front of the large wooden door. The engraving was a nice touch, enhancing the whole cozy lodge in rural America look. Dale sure hadn't wasted no time conning old Lady Quinn out of every dime to finance his childish endeavor of turning an old tobacco farm into a hunting preserve. Then again, he mused, a man who invested in killing things couldn't be all that bad

He didn't like emotions but couldn't help but smile as he angled the box slightly. He had his penchants, and was never satisfied with presentation, because presentation *was* key. Blue had always been her color; that's why he spent more than his frugalness preferred.

He didn't dare to look up or around in case Sam had gotten leery after his last gift and put a handful of those pesky cameras around like she had scattered along the old stone wall trail. That's why he walked in, from the north side where the trees were thickest, and the reason for wearing this blasted gray raincoat that concealed his more dominate traits when it made more noise than if he pulled up and honked the horn. He made sure to cut the phone lines, just to prove Quinn was not as smart as he thought he was.

Walking in, he spotted the black oval shape peering out from the eve of the barn and another pointing towards the kitchen door. Most home security these days were wireless and that meant an internet connection. No phone lines, no connection. He wasn't wise on thievery as much as stealthiness, but common sense told him to proceed with caution.

A part of him wished he could stick around, see her face when she opened her gift, but he needed to be smart, and being smart meant being far from Deer Creek Lodge before his gift was discovered.

He had hiked back to his truck, slid the raincoat into the lidded bucket, and aimed for town. No missteps he concluded. Half the town would be at church services and the other half, his half, would be here. Sitting at the Brick, where at least a dozen witnesses could see him, covered tracks better than a broom. By afternoon he would be clocked in, and no one would be the wiser.

Years had earned him patience and if he acquired them sooner he wouldn't be dealing with Samantha Carver right now. Not like this. If he had only waited a little longer he wouldn't have had to choose the other one that cool November night. He would have had the one he wanted. No one would miss a girl barely getting her feet wet in town. His only mistake was being impatient, taking one they all knew from the cradle. A mistake he never repeated.

That's how he learned to choose them, the one forgotten, not by making stupid, impulsive takes. Worth it at the time, he grinned evoking that memory, but hindsight was tricky like that, because that first blunder with the Quinn girl was trying to sneak back and bite him.

Insurance, that's what he needed, and a good distraction. This close to time again he was always a little itchier.

At ten thirty he stepped through the double doors of the Brick. For a Sunday he was surprised to see so many familiar faces, but the game was on and any man worth his weight was watching. Why else would he subject himself to silly games, if not to blend in?

Jake sat with his shoulders curled forward, cradling a beer. He sidled beside him, made small talk first. Jake was always too stupid to keep his thoughts to himself. One could learn a lot if he asked the right questions. Jake was an amateur, not near as tough as folks thought. Larry was right to keep a close watch on his son as he had. People called it abuse. That was laughable. Knocking a kid on the head for being an idiot wasn't abuse, it was discipline. He knew abuse and Jake Foster hadn't a clue what that was. He was a crier, because real men didn't watch stupid games and sulk in bars. Real men took what life handed them and used it to their advantage.

"Guess I missed all the excitement around here lately. Don Weaver says those feds have practically taken over the town and are staked out in the old news shop," he said, broaching the main topic.

"They are wasting time harassing us when they should be out looking for this maniac," Jake slurred angrily. "I saw them practically yank Tim Grimes from his truck as soon as he got into town yesterday afternoon." So they were suspecting a truck driver, he mused. That made sense. No wonder Don Weaver looked more sweaty than normal.

"And what does paying Old Man Pennington to mount a few bucks have to do with a bunch of dead women anyways?" Jake slurred out and took an angry drink.

"The taxidermist?" Now that was a riddle to ponder over, unless… He held his thoughts and cradled his own beer. Best not expose himself, acting as if he was more than a noisy bystander.

"Yeah, apparently that and Dad's disappearance back then makes me the number one dude to hound around here," Jake growled. "They questioned me for five hours, and look over there," Jake pointed the head of his bottle to a far corner.

He followed Jake's aim to two agents sitting stiffly in one corner getting their fill of Darlene's ribs and slaw.

"Them two follow me everywhere. I'm surprised they don't follow me to take a leak. They can't play cards worth crap," Jake saluted them with a grin. "Get you another beer. It's on them."

Jake had no idea the irony in that offer, but he did, and ordered that second bottle with a smile. A smart man could kill and still have the authorities buy him a beer.

"Look Nana, a present," Brody said excitedly as they pulled into the drive after church. Bouncing out of the truck, Sam laughed as he ran to the front porch and picked up the blue box and gave it a shake.

Quinn went to the passenger side door to help Nelly out of the back seat. "Looks like somebody is trying to make me look bad," he jested to Sam.

"You think she is the only woman worthy of presents here? Those fresh flowers in your room weren't picked out of the garden you know," Nelly added smugly.

"No ma'am. But she is the one having a birthday in a couple days." Quinn entwined his fingers into Sam's. He would never tire of that feeling. As they all walked towards the house, he took note of the blue box with twine wrapped into a shoe-tie bow. "Don't shake it bub. Could be breakable," he warned Brody.

"It says S.A.M.A.N.T.H.A." Brody read and Nelly huffed.

"You are sneaky," she looked to Quinn. "It's days before my birthday Henry."

"Really darling, it's not from me. Maybe your dad dropped it off." It seemed probable. "I don't care what he bought you, he can't top the present I gave you."

"And that would be..." She hiked a strong brow while her lips teased him to almost lose his concentration.

"Me," Quinn spread his arms, stirring a laugh. He missed her laugh, the rare sound he hoped to encourage with each passing day. It fed his bones, straight to the marrow.

"Well you do have a point," she purred and he couldn't resist any longer, pulling her in for a kiss.

"Oh open it already and keep that smooching to yourselves," Nelly quipped. Sam pulled the bow free playfully and lifted the lid partway to take a peek. Before her hands let go, Quinn sealed the box and kept it from crashing to the ground. He barely got a good look but it was clear someone was out to once again ruin a perfectly good day.

Quinn stood in the kitchen with Ron and Dorsey, all three staring at a blue box on the kitchen table. "He isn't afraid and that means we aren't even close to him," he pinned Dorsey with an accusing glare. If they didn't take this seriously, see Sam and his family protected, he would most certainly pack them up and leave within the hour.

"We don't know that for sure Mr. Quinn." Dorsey assured.

"Bull. She's become a target. You know it and I know it. Heck, she knows it even if she won't admit it," he swung his arm. He was trying to keep his voice down while Sam was upstairs with Brody. He would never get that mortified look out of his mind when acknowledgment and fear collided on her sweet face seeing what was left for just her. He wasn't sure he'd get that feeling in his gut to subside either. Sam was in danger, a maniac was targeting her.

Dorsey moved closer to the table. "Was this all that was in the box," he asked. Dorsey pulled out a pen from inside his jacket pocket and flipped open the box. Ron leaned in to take a regretful peek. The newspaper, a jawbone half peeking out, and the clear plastic seemed to keep it all intact.

"No, I added the skull myself," Quinn ripped. "What do you think? I took it the second I saw it." Quinn said.

"Brody? Nell?" Ron lifted his gaze, a ghostly look on his face.

"Aunt Nell got a look," Quinn winced sharing that fact. "Brody, thank the good Lord, didn't," Quinn paled. How would he explain to a seven-year-old the evils in the world? How would he ever reassure him of his safety when he now was questioning it himself?

"Excuse me gentlemen," Ron said removing his hat. "I need to go check in on Nell. Woman's had enough surprises for a lifetime."

"She's in the mud room," Quinn said

"She likes to clean when she's upset." The sheriff strolled out of the room and Quinn realized Sam had been spot on about those two.

"I've got a team on their way now," Dorsey said starring eerily into the evil on the kitchen table. "So, why her?" Good question. "Why would he send this to your fiancee'?"

"You boys must have a tap on the rumor mill here," Quinn shifted his stance, "and yet a killer is still out there."

"I saw the ring before she took the boy upstairs. Nice rock on a warden's salary." Dorsey said without implying much interest, just an observation.

"Had it a while. Saved longer than that," Quinn admitted. It was shameful to admit he put his first hundred dollars away in a special account when he was twenty, in hopes to come home a college grad with a career to win over the girl that captured his heart. Years down the road when Dale took that life and made it his own, Quinn added to it casually, figuring one day it would serve a good use. And it had. Now someone else was threatening to take all of that away from him. Quinn took a deep breath as the muscles between his shoulder blades tightened.

"Hey, look here," Dorsey urged.

"No thank you." Quinn wasn't looking into that box again.

"This newspaper has the date November 22, 1999. Isn't that about the day your…" Dorsey raised his head and got his answer. "We already have her remains, so this is someone else, but why the date?" Dorsey paced along the table. "Each missing report came within three days of Thanksgiving. I don't get the connection, but he's telling us something here." Quinn agreed and he feared he had the answer.

"Mrs. Quinn and your niece were close, weren't they?"

"Very, and Sam turns thirty-three on Friday," Quinn said as the air let out of him. "The discovery of his things didn't urge him into hiding. He isn't done." Quinn was crawling out of his skin searching for the best move. He had to get Sam and his family out of Milford and someplace safe.

"If the pattern holds true, a girl for every year, his next victim will have to be thirty-three.

"I think we have our pattern." But was it enough to find him before he made his next move?

"I hear my boys now. You go check on your family. I will see to getting this taken care of swiftly, but when you think she's ready, I need to speak to her. She's the key to it all."

CHAPTER NINETEEN

Quinn climbed the stairs, his unending prayers for her protection, combined with that for his family, was all he could do in the next five minutes. He paused just outside Brody's bedroom door. This whole day was a twister, a fast-moving mix of wonderful and horrible, both taking turns at smashing into him with a vile dominance to win the day.

Quinn ran his hands through his hair, gathered himself, and sent up one last prayer. "Whatever the cost Lord, let them be okay," and stepped into his old room.

Like a vision he once remembered, Sam sat cross legged on Brody's bedroom floor. She and Becky had spent hours singing the newest hits, painting their nails in a bed of magazines, neither knowing just how precious those idle days were back then. He had grieved himself dry at the loss of his niece. She had been his duty as the eldest Quinn, his focus when the loss of his own family came haunting, and his heart before he knew hearts could love more than just blood.

Sam was still here, only now playing trucks and cars with her son on a small, clothed mat with colorful roads and street signs. She had changed out of her Sunday clothes into jeans and what he now came to gather was her favorite gray sweater. A comfort item like Brody and that old raggedy red blanket it took Nelly and Sam two years to convince him to let go of. Lavender colored the underneath of her blue eyes, a powerful blend of fragile and resilient. She hadn't yet been to bed since her shift and he wished he could curl her up into his arms and let her rest there. Quinn sat down beside her and picked up one of Brody's trucks.

"Everything going okay?" she asked in a weary tone, not taking her eyes off her son. Of course she heard the voices from downstairs grow and was aware Dorsey's team had arrived to dust for prints and take the blue box to be further analyzed.

"It's going. More here, taking care of things," he never spoke in code before, but her soft nod said she understood his amateur attempt to say that the forensic team had arrived and was collecting as much evidence as possible. She ran a tender hand over her son's hair. Brody's revving noises faded away as he quickly grew bored of his trucks.

"Can I watch a cartoon?" Brody asked. After setting him up with a Spiderman movie, Sam and Quinn slipped into the hall. He put both hands on her sunken shoulders, kissed her forehead.

"Crime team is checking out our cameras and taking care of that…" What did you call a box with a skull wrapped in old newspaper dating the very day after your cousin disappeared? *The day of her own birthday.*

"The box," Sam called it. "Nelly must be scared to death. It's clear your family is a target." Quinn held his expression. She was the target and saying otherwise wasn't changing it.

Taking her hand, he ran a finger over the diamond encased in gold. He knew it was the one the moment he laid eyes on it. Not too tall to get in the way of her every day work, but worthy to catch the eye.

The three-quarter cut diamond embraced the diamond line petals. Love's desire, it was called, and Quinn was sold right there in the jeweler's store outside of Lexington. The diamond spoke of her as much as his want of her. All of Sam's sharp corners and brilliant curves cut in stone. The collision and twisting of the foundation spoke of their lives always entwining with oneanother's lives but never connecting. He had purchased the wedding band in matching fourteen carat white gold, which did connect in one wide cluster of two lives becoming one. It was their story, beginning to end, and worth all the years of cash thrown into a never forgotten hope that one day he would find a way to make her his.

"We need to take precautions now." He pulled her into him knowing that someone else had been hoping for her too. Quinn wasn't going to let that happen.

"I'm going to lock all the windows up here. Nelly and Ron will sit with Brody. The agent wants to talk with you." She nodded, knowing it couldn't be avoided.

"Everything from here on out, we do together. I will be right there the whole time." Sam looked up at him, touched his face with a feathery soft touch.

"Together, from here on," she whispered and it rattled his bones. He had never made a promise he didn't intend to keep.

The kitchen was a madhouse of strangers with gloves and cameras. Quinn's hand kept her steady as Dorsey offered her a seat in the sitting room.

"First, I don't want you to worry. I have men doing a perimeter check of the property and structures. A man will be outside watching over your family until this thing is over." Dorsey sat across from her and Quinn.

"Thank you. Nelly and Brody's safety are *our* top priority," Sam said with a lifted chin. He liked the sound of that. Despite what was weighing on her, Sam had accepted their new roles without hesitating.

"The cameras show nothing." Dorsey informed with a sigh.

"Nothing?" Quinn tilted his head. "Not even a vehicle or shadow?"

"They were disabled. Phone lines are cut."

"I thought they were wireless?" Sam asked.

"They were, but they need a connection. One of my guys found the cut line." Sam remained stiff, listening. Whoever left the box knew what he was doing.

Sam sunk lower in her seat. That was it, she silently pondered. Brody was getting a dog, a big one too. He always wanted one and dogs didn't let strangers close. Whatever this killer had in mind for her family, she hadn't a clue, but no way would she simply sat back, let Quinn be the only one seeing them all safe.

"Here's what we know as of now," Dorsey continued. "Maybe it will bring something to mind. An encounter or suspicion that could help us."

"I really don't know who could be behind all of this." No lie there and she tried thinking who she knew capable, even those she called friends.

"Maybe you do and don't even realize it, Mrs. Quinn. That gift was addressed to you." She flinched at the obvious.

"We have three potential suspects. Dates of abductions, access to the beetles we found, and opportunity. We also have a handful of secondary suspects. They either had opportunity or motive. We're getting close, but I'd like to leave a few agents here to be safe. And I think *you* should have someone with you at all times." Sam watched the men share looks with one another. What weren't they telling her?

"I work with the police force sitting over my head. I'm in the safest place in this town," she said as if they had to know. Quinn shot Dorsey a look before facing Sam.

"Darling, what he isn't telling you, and I need you to know, is the FBI doesn't think our family is this man's aim." Training prepared you for any kind of news but currently Sam couldn't see how she was a target. Had she not been right there the night Becky disappeared? If he wanted her, then why would he take someone who had a family?

"You're grasping at straws. It doesn't matter who is the target," She got to her feet. "I want Nelly and Brody watched at all times." They needed to focus on her family. She could take care of herself.

"I don't think you understand. There is a link between you and…"

"Mom," Brody appeared in the doorway quieting the agent immediately. "Are you okay?"

"Yes," she rushed to him, hoping he didn't hear what had been said. "And I'm ready for another race." With an arm around her son, Sam left Quinn and Dorsey to find a killer, she had a son to tend to.

CHAPTER TWENTY

He stared at the bag of cat food beside him as he drove out of town. Colder temperatures meant more trips to tend to the nature room. Kibble worked well enough this time of year but he made a mental note to buy it elsewhere for a while. Linda-Gail had asked for a third time why he bought cat food when he didn't own a cat. He winked a grin, made a quick excuse, and now the cute little blonde he had known since she was a toddler thought him a saint who bought dinner for all the strays in the county. What man didn't like being thought of as goodhearted? It was laughable.

The radio sang low and he tapped the steering wheel in cadence with the beat. Snow rained outside but so far it wasn't sticking to the warm pavement. Snow had always fascinated him and he had to admit even in his forties he felt stimulated by its bounty. Kentucky seasons were treasures he had been denied in his childhood and he looked forward to each one with fresh eagerness.

When he left home as a boy his aim was to get higher on the map. Somewhere further north were factories buzzed and streets crowded so busily a man could easily get lost in them. With two dollars in his pocket, one clean shirt, an empty gas tank that cold February day derailed that plan. So he found work, a place to lay his head while he saved up enough to move on. But one month turned into a year. A year turned into five. He hated roots, but found roots gave you a good alibi when needed.

The radio switched to a soft heartfelt ballad and he let his mind travel. Back to that day, the day he found his life's purpose. A man doesn't forget that day of days.

He had worked a few months for the florist, refueling his coffers, but a man needed more of a wage if he wanted to go anywhere. So he cleared his bank account of eight hundred dollars, packed his car and set out to put some distance behind him and just another stop on his way. He remembered the little gas station, the old coke machine that hummed next to the cigarette one. A habit he found repugnant and costly.

Filling his tank , he remembered the old rusty Ford pulling in beside him. The man behind the wheel was a mountain when he climbed out, stretched, and nodded his way friendly. Furniture and belongings in the back said this man was either new to Milford or passing through. As he listened to the stranger ask the gas attendant for directions to the old Maxwell place, he got confirmation.

Newcomers.

He popped the top of his Coke, pouring in the pack of peanuts just like his father used to, but before savoring the sweet stingy salty mix, she got out of the passenger side of the old Ford.

Waves of hair blew in the sun, catching his eyes first. When she begged for cash from the man, Ben Carver he later learned the stranger was, she kissed her father's cheek and ran inside the store. Why he followed he couldn't remember now. Maybe it was those legs or the way her simple blue dress revealed her womanly curves. He hadn't felt this taken, this mesmerized since a boy of seventeen when he first lured Patty Mitchell into her neighbor's shed.

She bought two Cokes, a zero bar and a pack of crackers. When they passed glances she floated him a smile that could knock a preacher off his high horse.

That was it, he knew what he wanted, and he got back into his vehicle and drove back to the rundown cabin on the back side of Bear Claw Mountain with a plan. He didn't care that she was young. Like Patty Mitchell, she wasn't so young she didn't know what she was doing, smiling at a man like that. Those sparkling sapphire eyes saw him in that brief encounter. Saw the real him, soul and guts and poor blood, and smiled anyway.

He spent a couple months planning it all out, down to the day she'd be his. If only he had practiced more patience that night, it all wouldn't have gone so wrong.

He chalked the whole experience up to learning from our mistakes. From means of thievery, taking his victims, to the very act of savoring his experience with them, each take grew with perfection. He learned to keep his secrets away from his front door. That's why he kept the old cabin when he had a perfectly good house in town. He refined his methods of simply using luck and circumstance to using modern technology as a means of selection. Then he grafted the perfect partner after Dana Bloom.

It had been an accident really. Finding the dead old owl near the cabin nearly picked clean, he knew it was a sign, and sweet little Dana his second victim, played the guinea pig while he worked out all the kinks in his system. He could have bought the bugs online for fifty bucks, but why leave a trail or waste hard earned cash when nature provided the solution readily. The old freezer left to rust in the cellar didn't work, so that too was a freebie. All he had to do was add the wire screens, Styrofoam bedding for the larva, and one solar panel attached to a couple of batteries ran the heating pads without fail. With research, time, and little effort, he had transformed the old basement cellar into the nature room. It was dark. They preferred dark. It was three years before he added the red lights to make his moving about safer. His first practice run was roadkill, a rabbit. It took twenty-six hours for the beetles to finish the flesh, but now the colony had grown and they had a preferred taste, much like his own.

He read once about a man who raised moths, planted them in his victim's throats. The movie was kind of good, but that was based on multiple men, not one. If the world only knew, he would be the most sought after killer of all time. It was thrilling to hold such knowledge inside you. He was far from done.

After parking on the worn, dirt drive he went inside the old single story cabin with water stained wood and rotted facing. His first job had paid for the run-down place. He could imagine the look on sweet Kelly's face if she only knew what really went on in her father's old hunting cabin.

He called into work on his way over. Service here was dead, another reason he liked the spot. The snow had shifted to flurries and he noted them dancing out of an ashen sky. He walked through the sitting room with dust and sheet-covered furniture and into the kitchen. It seemed strange to let the place look so dilapidated with new floors, but that was another measure of insurance no matter how it unnerved him to look at it.

He replaced the old boards that creaked and moaned with every step because the sound drove him insane. A man without his mind intact couldn't plan, execute, and succeed if not clear-headed.

He opened the old pantry door with chipped yellow paint, put his key into the lock, and entered the nature room. One disadvantage was the smell, the cold barely concealing it. He hadn't figured out a good remedy for that in all these years. But it kept nosy wanderers away better than locks and traps. He flipped on the light, sending an extra burst of crimson over the space. Tearing open the cat food bag, he dropped a handful of kibble through the small wire door. That should keep his accomplices thriving for now. Not too much, but just enough.

Back upstairs he felt the weariness of days of planning, of pretending, wearing on him. The cabin was freezing so he made quick work of striking kindling into flame to remedy that. He sat back in the old recliner, closed his eyes savoring the sweet crackling of fire, and smiled. She would be receiving her next gift. He had to drive all the way into Mt. Sterling, use the public computers to throw them off track. They thought he liked the north. They hadn't a clue what he liked, but they soon would.

CHAPTER TWENTY-ONE

Sam couldn't sleep. Just knowing someone out there capable of stealing life, targeting her family, she figured she would never sleep a wink again until this was all over. Outside her window the dark car sat it's motor running, it's exhaust's a ghostly white leaking into the night air. Those two agents could take a couple of the guest rooms where it made sense and they didn't have to freeze to death.

She slipped on her long-knitted sweater and crept downstairs. Cocoa or tea, she debated mentally as she stepped into the quiet kitchen.

He sat with his head down, arms stretched out across the table. A man in the throes of solving problems, she measured. Below his gaze, a map, markings in red and black splattered chaotically. He didn't look up and she didn't go further.

He bore the weight of protector and for a moment she wanted to take that in too. Admire the man she loved and who loved her without conditions, a man who admitted to loving her most of her life. It wasn't fair to think that after all these years, the repeated losses, the aches to her heart, everything she ever wanted sat just across the way and now that too might be lost to her.

"You'll be 33 soon," he didn't look up but knew she was there. His voice sounded weary and she had to admit, she felt equally drained.

"Thinking what to get me," she draped an arm over his shoulder. She didn't want to think about killers and bodies, she wanted to enjoy every second before they blinked out.

"Thinking how to keep you safe and stop this man."

"I could tell you that you're not a cop. I could tell you to get some sleep and let them do their job," she said.

"Well thank you for not telling me any of that." He refused to look at her, his gaze focused on the map before him.

"So," she moved to his side. "What is all of this?"

"This is all the places they went missing. The red indicates they have been identified." Sam noted there was a lot of red.

"Cocoa?" She didn't want to think about those women, what they went through. She didn't want to think about what Becky went through. If Quinn looked close enough he would see how many tears she had already shed thinking about them.

"The victims had that in common." Sam stiffened. He wasn't talking about cocoa.

"They all shared your birthday." He said it with such conviction it sent a chill over her. Her arm slipped from his shoulder. Those words nixed any hope that this was all just some bad dream.

"All, but one," the words fell out. "Oh, Quinn." Now she understood and no guilt ever stabbed so deeply. Becky had been a mistake. Becky could have lived. Quinn turned, collected her hands.

"We can't change what has happened, but we can prevent what's coming." He got to his feet and wrapped both arms around her. "Your dad is coming back to stay for a few days." He slowly lifted his gaze to her.

"Brody will like that now that school is almost out for Thanksgiving break." She backed out of his hold and looked up to him. "It's my fault, isn't it? That Nelly lost…"

"No, it was his doing. He could have planned to take you both for all we know." He meant to ease her liability, but it didn't work.

"Do you think this man will really try to come after me?"

"That won't happen. I waited a long time for you Samantha, nothing but God himself can stop me from having you," he reached for her hand and she gave it.

"Promise?"

"Promise." And she believed him.

"Part of me wants to lock you in your room until this all is over," Quinn admitted.

"And the other part?"

"Still wants to lock you in your room, but with me in it." She liked that forwardness that once unnerved her and wished it was all that easy.

"We have to find him," she said with a fresh readiness. "Before it happens again." No, she wouldn't dwell on the possibilities of that night long ago. She would focus on the now, as Quinn said, and help anyway she could.

"We need cocoa. It might be a long night," she stepped from his hold and fetched a pan to warm the milk. His eyes dissected her moves, expressions. If he was trying to read her thoughts, he would be hard-pressed doing so. She knew how to close them off. She was a dispatcher. It was time to focus on who *he* was.

"We should consider everyone." She nodded as she removed milk from the refrigerator. "I hate to admit it, but I agree with Dorsey."

"Quinn I can't think of anyone I know in this town capable of..." She stopped, poured the milk into a pan, and returned the jug to the refrigerator.

"We are thinking who here is capable, but a man like this is well-rehearsed in disguising himself. Think as far back as you can. Who stands out? Is there an old boyfriend who couldn't handle rejection, or someone who seems to always be around but shouldn't be? Any guy interested since you moved here that you turned down?"

As the milk heated, she turned to him. "Quinn. The women lived in a two-hundred-mile radius, so I agree he could be a local, but perhaps not *that* local. It's a small town so like every single woman here I've had to deliver a few rejections. Ed has been the most persistent but has never been forward or acted in a way that suggest he might want to step up his game into the serial killer mode," she said knowing that bothered him.

"I'm aware of that, but other than wanting to punch him in the throat, I don't think he fits the profile either," Quinn shot back. He crossed his arms and put on a mischievous grin.

"Let me throw out some names, you say the first thing that comes to mind."

"Not sure of your methods Warden, but go ahead," she searched out a wooden spoon and the cocoa mix next.

"Jake?" Sam shot him a glare. "What? We both know he is considered the main suspect." Quinn threw up his hands in defense. He knew she would react to that. That's why he wanted to get Jake out of the way.

"Jake loved her. He's dating too. He might be a smart mouth with a bad history, but I bet my life he's innocence. He was a wreck, and I was there Quinn, he ran after her until he couldn't any more."

"I know," Quinn dropped his gaze shamefully. "What about Mr. Florence?"

"Really?"

"He and the Mrs fight, destroy things. You forget I hear what goes on about too," Quinn added. "Kevin Florence loves to hunt and has about four mounts on his wall. He is the right age and lives down the road from your dad."

"And he adores his wife," Sam snapped back and he knew just what drove Kevin Florence to busting furniture.

"Guess some men like when a woman's all riled up." He chuckled when she narrowed her eyes at him. "What about Tim Grimes or Don Weaver?"

"They both have asked me out, yes, but they have everyone. Neither seemed bothered by a no from me or any other woman around her. They are kind of used to refusals."

"What about Bob Cane, Mack Dawson, or Freddie McGuire? They work at the power plant and each fit some of the traits the profiler suggests."

"Bob is strange, too smart for his own good, but his son is a deputy. It would be hard to hide a body for three months or better before taking the remains up on our mountain." Quinn swallowed in her brash comment. He hated she had been doing a little investigating herself, but part of him was glad they didn't have to address that part of it too.

"I Googled it," she said snarky. "I know beetles help investigators and forensic scientists, and now I know how long it takes them to do what they do," she shivered just as she had when reading the information.

Quinn considered what they knew so far. "He's close. I know he is. That's what bothers me the most. Who to trust," he said palming the back of his neck and the tension there.

"He kills by birthday, not traits like hair color, skin color." Quinn stood as she stirred the pan on the stove and reached for a bag of marshmallows overhead. He placed a hand on her waist, and pulled the bag from the top shelf.

"Well, what about the dates?"

"Dates?" He needed to focus.

"The agent said dates. Like a pattern. Is there a connection to the dates?" She was barely audible.

"Only that they shared birthdays."

"A serial killer who takes trophies, one for every year," she said as if speaking to herself. Quinn growled but didn't argue that her working brain remained intact even after knowing what this man had in mind for her.

"At least give me some of those marshmallows to sweeten this conversation." She turned and poured them both a cup of overly heated cocoa and added extra to his cup.

"He likes bugs, picks them by age, and no other similarity they can pin down." He took a sip of the steaming cup, swallowed, and watched her do the same. "He's a clean freak. Traces of something Dorsey said led them to that. They also mentioned yellow paint chips, old paint so nothing they can follow up on." He reached over and took her hand. "And he isn't done. None of this digging around seems to worry him."

"He's killed her over and over," Sam mumbled, her hands steeling. "*He's killing me over and over,*" she corrected and fisted her stomach in the knowing.

"He's not getting a chance," Quinn said between clenched teeth. "But your thinking is on track, though I wish it weren't." Quinn shook his head, an ache forming behind his eyes. "Let's piece this together from scratch; time is not on our side here Sam."

"So he either is self-employed, retired, or his schedule changes regularly." Quinn hesitated and let each word sink in fully. "I'm surrounded by cops all day, and I read a lot of mysteries. Think about it. How else would he have opportunity at random times to take girls? If he is neat and clean as you say, he needs money. Poor as dirt isn't just an expression. So he isn't some hermit in the hills." She looked serious, not shaken, and add found an angle even Dorsey hadn't considered.

"Okay Ms. Lansbury, go on," Quinn encouraged taking in her every word.

"Think about our town. Other than those working at the grocery store or gas station, who else has no set schedule to follow? It's easy really. Tim and Don aren't killers. That would take more effort than those two are willing to exhaust," she rolled her eyes. "Most of the men here either work at the mill with my father or they work for the power company across the river. Their schedule...changes. It's called a..." She snapped her fingers adorably struggling for the word.

"DuPont Shift." It made perfect sense. He sat his cup down and took hers from her hands and did the same before sweeping her off her feet. "You're a genius." And beautiful, and loving, and, he wanted to keep adding.

"What did I say?" She giggled softly.

"Profiler says our guy is between forty and fifty-five. Not real retirement age, but a smaller range to consider. The sheriff already checked on all retired and self-employed men, and they all have alibis except the truck driver and a warden south of here, but no one thought of swing shifts. Now we just have to find locals who had those days off and if they coincide with every girl or possibly the list we made of those captured on your wildlife cameras."

"It can't be that easy."

"Or it could be. I'm calling Dorsey now." Quinn grabbed his cell from the table and dialed the number. The faster they caught this man, the faster his life could finally begin.

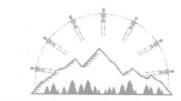

CHAPTER TWENTY-TWO

Quinn wasn't fully awake but he managed to put on a pair of jeans and a shirt and slipped into the kitchen as soon as Nelly had awakened him with worried eyes and a tone laced in real concern. "She has been at it for hours and barks every time I come close to the kitchen," Nelly warned, saying it was best he come to see for himself.

He didn't know what to expect but he surely hadn't been imagining the scene he walked into. Her apron matched the flour coated counter tops. He could see by the looks of pies and a large chocolate cake cooling on the table she had been at it for a while.

Something dark bubbled on the back of the stove. From her chaotic twisted hair to her winged pace, it appeared the calm rational dispatcher who melted under his hand, talked about death like a veteran investigator last night, was now coming to grips with the reality of her situation. Today was Thanksgiving, and with that came alarm instead of thankfulness God was giving her another year of life.

On bare feet Quinn stepped further into the kitchen. No light flaunted through the three windows over the kitchen sink. He hadn't checked the time when Nelly came barging into his room but he knew it was still early. "Sam dear, what are you doing?"

"I'm cooking a dang turkey what's it look like?" The oven beeped and she slid in the large roasting pan he assumed held the turkey she was speaking of. She slammed the oven door, rattling plates and glasses in the cabinets.

Quinn approached with caution as she now was chopping, or for a better word, hacking the potatoes. "Don't say it Henry."

"Okay. I won't." Their first true Thanksgiving together and she was on the edge of panic. Quinn couldn't blame her for worrying. She was a target. He had to admit he lay awake late into the night with similar dread. What Sam needed was a distraction, something to take her mind from all of this. Hopefully his plan for doing just that was just the medicine she needed to switch back to normal again.

"It's our first real Thanksgiving." Emotion drove her words. "Brody and Nelly need normal. I need normal," her voice told him she was near bursting. "This is normal. Tomorrow I could be... dead!" Her voice hitched.

Quinn reached her side and tenderly took her elbow. There it came. The flood, the tears she hated, let loose by his simple touch. With one hand Quinn gripped the knife and with the other he pulled her into him.

"It's okay. Shhh," he soothed, tossing the knife to the sink in the safe distance. Caressing her hair, the light scents of jasmine and honey that always rested there filled his breath. He tightened his embrace, just shy of breaking her he figured.

"I don't want to think some maniac wants another body, mine or anybody else's. I don't want to have a birthday and I don't want to know that after tomorrow I have three-hundred- and sixty- four more days of wondering, waiting." She buried her face deep into him and cried.

"I won't let that happen," he promised. "We have to have faith. God didn't bring us this far to let evil stop us now." Quinn believed that wholeheartedly. She was a testimony of strength, of fortitude. She was everything he could see ahead and everything he remembered before. He would protect her, or die trying.

He let her cry on his shoulder. She gripped his sleeves as if they were life vests keeping her afloat. When she felt nearly cried out, Sam leaned back and brushed away her damp face. "Henry, promise me something."

"Anything my dear," he said running his hands up and down her bare arms.

"If this man wins, if something happens to me, promise you will take care of Brody and Nell. Promise they will be the most important purpose in your life as they have been in mine." Those begging blue eyes penetrated him.

"I promise to love you for the rest of our lives, and Brody and Nell, and you, will always be my everything." He kissed her forehead and lifted her chin to look at him. "Now let's get this meal put together." He kissed her warm damp face, one cheek and then the other. He placed a soft peck on the tip of her nose before brushing his lips against hers. "I'll carve today, and tomorrow we're celebrating."

"Celebrating?" she wiped the back of her hand over her face.

"We're getting ribs from the Brick and Aunt Nelly is already talking about a cake. Birthdays are for celebrating, for family and friends, and not worrying." That brought out an innocent flush to her cheeks. No maniac was going to come between what was his. No maniac was going to ruin this special day of all days for her.

"Is that smart? I mean how can we even think to live normal when..."

"You have every police officer and agent in a two-hundred-mile radius either searching or here watching over all of you. And don't count me out princess. I may wear green but can go white knight when I have to," he flaunted stirring a weak grin out of her.

"Dorsey is working on it and if your theory is sound, all the men that work at the plant are clocking in tomorrow. They are on a seven-day shift. If our guy works for the power company, and Dorsey feels you are on to something there, he's sticking to routine. So what do you say beautiful? Want to put on a pretty dress and let our family and friends come over and celebrate tomorrow?"

"What about this monster?"

"Who thinks you're working, when instead, you're going to be here with me and Brody, eating cake." He watched her face shift in seeing the sense in his words. "Brody will have six men watching over him, even Clark will check in." With that, he could see she believed it was possible, that no monster could get close. Now all he had to do was make sure of that.

"I guess I can find something nice to wear," she said.

"I like blue, if you're taking suggestions." She chuckled and kissed him.

She wore the blue dress, because Quinn liked blue. She appreciated him trying to make the day anything but just another day of waiting until she could have a green light to live again. While she waited for everyone to arrive, Sam snatched a piece of yesterday's leftover turkey and went to the sitting room to check on her site.

As she clicked through a list of junk emails, she thought about what Quinn had said yesterday. She needed to have faith, but that was something she had struggled with for a long while. *"He is my rock, and my fortress, and my deliverer,"* she spoke out loud the familiar psalm. *"My God, my strength, in whom I trust."*

Trust. She was learning to trust.

It had been their first true Thanksgiving, and now they would celebrate a birthday together. Quinn had given the Thanksgiving prayer, which Sam found as attractive as the man shamelessly praised God for Him many blessings. Through all of this, Quinn thanked God and now, she was beginning to see how better it was to focus on the blessings, than whatever the day brought.

"So, have you set a date yet?" Ron asked as he and Quinn stepped into the room. Out of uniform he looked younger, slimmer, and Sam could see why those big puppy dog brown eyes kept Nelly smiling. It was beautiful to witness.

"Tomorrow if she would let me, but I'm sure she has fancies to consider." Sam laughed at Quinn's remark. She needed no fancies, and if her life was to be cut short, she wasn't wasting any time loving him while she could. Henry Quinn was a beautiful man, both inside and out. He loved her, her son, and God. Made no qualms about it either. The butterflies that she thought were natural for all women had grown into sparrows.

"I'm not into fancies," she replied.

"I can meet you at the courthouse in an hour." He teased causing another round of laughter.

"No eloping. It will be here with your family and friends," Nelly quipped.

"Quinn says I'm his best man. That means I give him my mom and get to hold her ring." Brody added proudly.

"Glad to see you so excited to give me away," Sam teased and kissed Brody's cheek. She wished her father had been here tonight but he had to work the late shift again. Sam made a mental note to see he had all his favorites waiting for him when he returned.

"Christmas weddings are nice," Agent Cooper added. "I married my Maria on Christmas."

"We can't take the Lord's spotlight. We can have a small quiet ceremony here," Sam replied.

"Tomorrow?" Quinn lifted a brow tugging his lips with it into a greedy smile.

"Give me at least a week. I am getting a dress and you are wearing a suit at least."

"I'll plan the meal after you make a list of invites. Shoot, that doesn't give me much time. Maybe Kelly can help with flowers and Stella hasn't decorated a cake in years but I bet for you two she would step out of retirement. And Ron can see about chairs," Nelly turned to the sheriff midway to filling his mouth with cranberry jelly and turkey combined. Nothing wasted under Nelly's watch and Sam was certain if Ron kept coming over his cholesterol might need to be checked.

"The ones at the fellowship hall are newer. Fifty maybe." Ron nodded obediently. He obviously liked being included as much as Nelly liked having something big to plan.

Quinn reached over and pulled Sam's hand to his lips and kissed it. "One week," he said.

"One week," she stared back, her heart anticipating being this man's wife.

"Oh that must be Darlene now," Nelly stood.

"Let's go help Sheriff," Quinn said getting to his feet. "I think Aunt Nell ordered enough for the whole town."

Sam could smell the BBQ long before she saw the woman. Like a woman with a purpose, Darlene marched in the sitting room looking like a mad hen in a rainstorm. She was a stout woman, rich brown eyes that stalked her boundary efficiently. Her dark hair was sprinkled in gray, giving her the strong contrast of a woman capable of handling her own.

"So, you two lovebirds figuring on marrying without me cooking or what?" Darlene said bluntly cocking a healthy hip to one side.

"We just ordered three hundred dollars worth of your cooking," Quinn said sounding a bit put off.

"Don't sass me young man." Darlene waved a chubby finger in warning. "I remember when you were in pull-ups packing dry sticks and pretending they could shoot bullets."

"Nelly is planning everything but the dress. I'm sure she would love it if you were willing to help out," Sam quickly added. "I bet you could tell me a lot of stories about this one," Sam winked to Darlene.

"If these walls could talk, I'd have to wear hear plugs. And I'll see Nelly has her duties, and I'll have mine." Sam didn't doubt it one bit. Darlene stomped off with a slight hitch in her stride. In less than three seconds she and Nelly were already talking in higher pitches and sounding like old church ladies at a fellowship meal.

"So you want to hear stories about me," he flirted Sam a grin. "Not as exciting as you might think."

"More than my stories," she said.

"I'll go see if Brody has fallen asleep watching Iron Man again."

Sam smiled in his exit. How did she get so lucky? Turning her attention back to her laptop, she scrolled her social media page, hit a couple likes to let the world know she still existed, then flipped back to her emails. The Whitley's had sent her more pictures of their newest adventure in Canada. She really liked Crystal and other than Connie, hadn't really let herself connect with other women since Becky.

An email marked the Mt. Sterling public library popped up. SAM QUINN, library dues. That was four counties away and Sam rarely went to the local library as it was, once a month to replenish her to be read pile. Perplexed she clicked and opened the email.

The blue hues varied from bold to unexacting pale. *The Happy Birthday Samantha Carver* would have made her smile if not for the eerie font, Snap ITC, a gothic bleeding typeface option she too had on her desktop.

A mountain faded in the background with a crimson x over the hand script word, *mine*. Squinting she noted how familiar the standing timber and old worn trail looked. She noted the navy blue box, similar to the one her son lifted from her porch steps. She clicked on the arrow teasing to be clicked. The box's top lifted in mechanical motion to reveal a picture of her taken not long after her father brought her to Milford to live. Her hair was sun kissed, streaked with ivory strands and a length she had never returned to since that first month of school. It drew too much attention. Terror gripped her spine, squeezing until she felt herself bend to its power. She needed no explanation, the message was clear.

Quinn stepped back into the room and their eyes locked instantly. "Quinn," her voice trembled so harshly it took over the rest of her. If she was at her desk, she would have called it in as a crash survivor in shock.

CHAPTER TWENTY-THREE

It didn't take long to learn the tree hugger had found yet another way to ruin his plans. His blood ran hot as he drove off the mountain through the slush and cold. Temper licked him roughly, but he didn't buckle under pressure. They hoped he would, but if they did their job right, they'd know some years he overshot.

Lacy Baker had been sixteen, and that one taught him to regroup and accept he might miss his mark, but that didn't mean he'd miss the kill.

Looking out the water-slick window, he noted the familiar silhouette standing outside. He liked the red head, her punch and flair, but she talked way too much. Normally he waved her off when she neared, enticing him with those swaying hips and overly generous wildflower scents. A cold night for stalking, and he wasn't alone, but part of the thrill was being smarter. They wouldn't expect it, and that made him smile.

"Hey," he said as he approached. "Locking up for the night?"

"Yeah. No one wants to come out anyways with all this crazy killer on the loose talk. It's bad for business, you know." Felicity's purple blouse blew in the cold breeze giving him a taunting peek of her endowments.

"Need a walk home?" He strode beside her. He had known her long enough she wasn't worried about serial killers in dark corners with him at her side. The thought made him stand taller.

"If you'd like," she said casually. "I guess I should pay more attention and not walk alone, in case."

"I agree. A woman as beautiful as you has no business wandering alone regardless." He complimented, which earned him a sly grin.

"You alone tonight?"

"Yeah. Well except for those two," he pointed towards a black SUV. "Follow me everywhere," he blew out a sigh in a white puff.

"You know Felicity, you've dated every man in this town and yet, missed one. I didn't take you as one who looked over such a skilled and eligible bachelor. How about I buy you a drink?"

"Single huh," her head cocked sideways giving him a second look. "Why not Jake," she flirted him a grin, "Why not."

CHAPTER TWENTY-FOUR

She could finally relax a little. If what everyone said was true, she had surpassed the mark, the one that made her a target. Sam was thirty-three and a day. Ron believed the killer was on the run, knowing they were only edging closer to him.

She brushed her hair back over her shoulder and felt as if her happy-ever-after was now possible. As she sat behind her desk while the rest of the town slept, she thumbed through the magazines Connie not-so-subtly left by the decades old coffee pot. She had worn white once, but as she flipped through the second magazine, suddenly the idea of a long gown oddly appealed to her.

Just yesterday Sam wouldn't have thought about wedding plans or long ivory dresses trimming her waist, but as she sat behind a fortress guarded so heavily, she finally let the whole idea of being Henry's wife bubble up inside her. He was timber steady and a constant reminder that God did have plans for her. The idea of more children suddenly birthed a fresh joy she hadn't even considered until now. Brody would love a sibling, and Henry holding a child, their child, warmed her heart.

"A daughter," she laughed out loud. "A daughter perhaps with her father's passions and steadiness, and her drive to work hard for the things you wanted."

Footfalls outside drew her attention to the clock. Two a.m. was terribly early for a check-in. Despite knowing security systems and agents sat on the other side of the door, Sam bristled as apprehension swallowed down her happy feel-good moment. She glanced at the camera and let out a breath she hadn't realized she was holding until now when David pressed his face to the door in childlike fashion. She needed to calm down and trust what Ron said was true. No one hoping to snatch her away from her dreams would be caught dead within five hundred feet of where she was right now.

David turned the lock when she waved him in, entering with one very drunk Mack Dawson at his side.

"Mack, you're the last person I ever imagined David dragging down here," Sam said stupefied.

"Well he and Jake had a contest," David explained. "Jake is sleeping it off at home where this one should have been."

"Ol' Dave here could have taken me home to sleep it off too, but no, bump into a few cars and you get your first night in jail." Mack swayed to the right as he was led down the little hall, past the vending machine, and into a cell to sleep it off.

"Set off every vehicle alarm in town and I find you urinating on public property, and it does," David added moving down the short, darkened hall. Sam almost snickered. Mack Dawson was a saint as a citizen, always helping when he could. His need for cleanliness a little OCD, but Sam had heard stories that he moved here to escape a poor upbringing. Nothing like living in squalor to make you want a clean slate.

"Don't worry Sam, this one won't cause you any trouble. Vivian down at the Brick said he just can't hold his liquor." Sam wasn't worried. Mack was a kitten, shy as a field mouse, and since no calls had come in all night, his company would be appreciated.

"I'm not arresting him, just letting him sleep it off before he can drive home," David added adjusted his belt.

"What about Jake," because part of her always worried about Jake Foster like a mothering hen.

"Oh, some suit drug him home. I think they have taken a liking to him. Lucky pain in the rear," he smarted. "I've got to file the report, because you know how Ron is about filing reports," David laughed, "Want me to go fetch you a snack, fresh coffee maybe?" Sam lifted a thermos and grinned. She was drinking less coffee and more cocoa this time of year.

"Did Mr. Romantic pack that or Nelly? Cause if that's Nelly's hot cocoa, I want some." David begged. Sam poured him a cup and ignoring the report for now, David took a seat across from her desk. Mack Dawson began snoring and they both chuckled.

"I can't believe he let you come in to work, considering..." David winced at his own words.

"Let me? We aren't married yet," she said drawing a laugh out of him. "I'm in the safest place in the world and Brody and Nell have three house guests who would fight a running sawmill for them." It was true the men were no longer strangers and adored Brody as much as they did home cooked meals.

"I'm glad you said yes," David said over the brim of steamy Styrofoam in his hand.

"Me too," Sam replied. Would she ever get used to the idea of Henry being hers? She thought not. She couldn't hide the smile it brought her.

"He has had it bad for you since we were kids. I don't know how he managed to hold it that long. Heck if it were me I would have found me another gal to pester." That wasn't true and Sam scolded his lie. David's wife was gone, married to another, and here he was still as in love with her as the day they married. "You two got your own little fairy tale going on," David added.

"I truly never knew," Sam sipped at her own cup.

"And they call our species absentminded," he rolled his eyes playfully. "Maybe I should have taken pointers," David lowered his head, obviously thinking about Chrystal.

"I'm sorry David. I know Chrystal hurt you leaving like that. That's not on you."

"We fought, a lot, bills, kids, bigger house. You know the stuff people fight about." Sam didn't know. In her marriage to Dale arguments were of a different nature and though she expected quite a few battle of words in her future with the handsome Henry Quinn, she imagined making up would be just as fun.

The phone rang and Sam sat down her cup. "Sorry David, duty calls." He saluted her before getting to his feet and going back out and up the old courthouse stairs to the sheriff's office. Now he would have to do that report, she mused.

"911, Where's your emergency?"

A few hours later Sam let her arms drop to her sides and felt the adrenaline leave her body. The feed store fire had awakened up half the town, which included all the volunteers needed to fight the inferno. Sam's ear burned with static bouncing across channels and her fingers logged every word.

Mack had awakened about five. She had gotten him some water and aspirin. Another two hours before Cindy was due to arrive and she and Quinn could have a few minutes to themselves before toting Brody off to school. This was the kind of normal she had been ready to fall back too.

"So you figure they're going to put poor Jake in jail for that mess involving your family?" Mack hollered out from the next room.

"I hope not." Sam replied. Standing, she gave her body a stretch and went to lean on the cell room door. Mack looked a mess sitting there on the sunk in little cot, head in his hands. He usually wore trousers, a button-up that always looked to be freshly ironed, but right now he looked like a man who drank too much and slept too little.

"Jake had no part in any of that, then or now," Sam said. He lifted his head, hair tussled in every direction. Why had he never married, she thought. Mack was handsome, had a care for those around him, and never once stepped on the other side of good.

"What, you don't think him capable?" Mack chuckled in a rusty voice. "Women never find the good looking ones capable and they're usually the ones."

"You have always been a nice-looking man too. Doesn't mean you're a killer does it?" she said sharply. Mack threw up his hands.

"Geez Sam. Ask a question and get the stink eye. Is that jerk deputy friend of yours coming back to release me or not?"

"Deputy Cane or the sheriff will be in shortly. They're still working on the fire over at the feed store." She snubbed him to get back to her station as the next call came in. Mack was a lousy drunk.

"911 where's your emergency?"

Nothing could have prepared her for this call, but Sam did her job, unattached, despite fearing the worst in the back of her mind. Had another victim paid the price for her to sit in this chair another day?

From what she knew so far passing information between responders, the body was found less than two miles from her house on the side of the road. If Pete Taulbee hadn't been forced to get out and personally move the fallen log across the roadway himself, no one would have ever found her.

A red head was all the chatter that filled her ears as her fingers worked busily to keep a log until oddly, all the officers went silent. Sam swallowed back a huge wave of guilt. Inwardly she knew there was only one five-foot seven red head in heels that lived in Milford. Why else would all radios have gone silent if not for it being one of their own?

Her phone rang but just then another emergency call came in so she sent Quinn a text that she was safe and loved him. He had to know what had happened, considering he made a point to follow the waves.

More than likely he would drive out, meet with Dorsey and Ron. It was too close to home she knew. Quinn would definitely be in the middle of it. A shiver ran over her and the need to get home soon overwhelmed her.

When Cindy rolled into work, even she seemed to be prepared for the long day ahead by the wildly alert look on her sunless face. "Guess you heard," Sam said standing.

"Half the town has by now. A fire and then a murder. What's happening to our peaceful little town?" Cindy unwrapped her homemade timber brown shawl and worked out of her jacket when someone knocked on the outside door. The monitor revealed Agent Vick and Cindy let him in. It must be a requirement to wear black to be a federal investigator. Sam was glad Connie never enforced a dress code here.

"Mrs. Quinn, I need to go join my supervisor and have strict orders to tell you to stay put until the warden gets here to pick you up." Vick's freshly grown facial hair blinked light red hues against the dull lighting.

"Thank you Vick for letting me know." Now she would have to wait even longer to get back to the lodge. Nelly would be cleaning like a woman on fire and a gut full of worry if she didn't get home soon." Sam began collecting her things and moved them aside for Cindy to take her place.

"I would like to go home too in case anyone cares," Mack yelled out from the back again.

"Let me call David and see what I can do." After calling David to confirm, Sam and Cindy pulled the extra set of keys from the desk drawer and unlocked Mack's cell. David wasn't pressing charges and for that Sam was glad. Mack had never done anything to break the law in all his years. David surely was only keeping him safe to sleep off his foolishness.

Sam stood back as the radio began filling with chatter. Cindy put the earpiece to her ear and immediately went to work.

"Mack, you should go." He nodded and aimed for the door. Technically he didn't need to be hearing anything said between officers and responders.

"I know a lot is happening. I don't have children, but if you need a lift home, back to your son…"

Her mind on Felicity, her worries for her family, Sam quickly answered with added sympathy, "Of course Mack." Quinn could be hours and Mack was right there. Brody and Nell needed her and Sam didn't like that so many calls were coming in at once.

A gasp drew her attention to the nerve center. Tears pooled then slowly ran down Cindy's face. Sam took a breath and waited.

"It was Felicity. Someone strangled and dumped her." Sam jerked. "Who would hurt Felicity?" Sam went to comfort her. This wasn't right. She shook her head. Sam may have hated her as long as she knew her, but she would have never wished death on her.

"I don't like the smell of this town today," Mack said. "Let's get going so you can get back to your family where it's safe," Mack stated, placing a comforting hand on her shoulder. "I know that warden fella would want you somewhere he won't have to worry about you." Mack turned to Cindy. "Does this door lock? If so, lock it behind us. Whoever did this could be right under your noses."

Sam agreed with his logic and appreciated how much he was considering both of them. Mack lived here too and most certainly didn't want to see his friends and neighbors in harm's way.

After leaving Cindy behind the locked door Sam followed Mack to his truck. She tried Quinn's cell, but it kept going to voicemail. So much of the road to her house didn't get service. She started to leave him a message, tell him Mack was taking her home, but Mack bumped into her.

"Sorry, I guess I haven't slept long enough. I'm kind of new to being an idiot," he admitted guiltily

When they reached the old truck, Mack reached for the driver's door handle. "Here, let me help you. This one sticks sometimes." With a jerk, he opened the driver's side door. Sam shot him a confused look. "Sorry, but I'm not sure my night is completely worn off. I'd hate to get sick while driving you. I'd have the whole police force ready to lock me up for good," he smiled innocently.

It made sense she thought, and she didn't like being a passenger anyways, so she climbed inside. She quickly started the engine and turned up the heat as he climbed in the passenger side.

"Nell can fix you some coffee before you try driving home," she said as she put the truck in drive. "It might help." She added but her mind was on Quinn and Brody and all those helping to find out what happened to Felicity Brown.

"That's kind of ya." He said giving a belly a rub. She hoped he didn't get sick. "I couldn't help but overhear some," Mack stared out the window. "I saw her...last night at the Brick. She was with Jake." Sam ruffled. Surely Jake would be with Sheryl, not Felicity. She gave Mack a quick glance but he was focused on the cold wintry scene outside.

"Surely you don't think he..." She couldn't bring herself to finish the thought.

"Jake, no." Mack said flatly. "That one hasn't got it in him to kill. Too soft." Sam pulled out onto the road and agreed but the way Mack spoke so forwardly had caught her by surprise.

"He also doesn't fit the profile," Sam shared. She really didn't like to think Jake was always a number one suspect.

"I read the papers, but I know they are hiding details from the public. Good plan. Helps sift through suspects I guess."

"Do you think whoever killed all those women did that to her?" It was nice to think out loud and Mack didn't seem as timid as Cindy on the subject.

"I do. I say Felicity was to throw the police off his trail," Mack said without hesitation. Sam darted him another glance.

"Really? How do you mean?" It could be possible.

"If I was the murderer and killed all those women, I would," Mack turned and met her eyes with a pair of seductive blue eyes. His short sandy hair had always looked the same. He always looked the same, with exception of that pining look. She focused back on the road. Of course Mack wouldn't actually do that, but his words held merit. If the FBI and detectives were getting closer, poor Felicity could have been a distraction. But Felicity was a year younger. Yet there was the feed mill fire, she collected. Distracted, she tightened her grip on the steering wheel to keep herself grounded. She'd be home soon. She could think more about it then.

"But you're not a murderer." Sam replied and turned down Hemmingway Street instead of the main road. The shortcut would get her home a lot faster.

"I did kill a couple of cats, and an owl." When she looked his way this time, Mack's serpentine grin made her skin crawl. Why he felt to share that with her, she hadn't a clue.

Suddenly Quinn's words hit her. Though the FBI wasn't sure the murderer was connected to the power plant, Quinn believed the connection was sturdy and all the local men at the plant were currently on shift, except the one riding in the passenger seat beside her.

Alarms rang through every cell in her body and she tried to keep her hands from trembling on the steering wheel. Maybe she was overreacting, being jumpy. Mack Dawson was no murderer she tried reminding herself. David had even put him in a cell seeing him no threat either. No threat, because everyone knew Mack, and though he hadn't many close friends, he had no enemies either.

"I thought your shift started yesterday." Sam queried in a tone as calm as she could manage as more and more of the profile of a killer began syncing with the man beside her. David's brick house was just fifty yards away. He shift was technically over, unless they pulled him in to help, she reminded herself. Small town deputies did have to step in when more than one emergency occurred.

Still, it was an idea. She could make an excuse. Or perhaps she could slip the cell phone from her pocket and pretend to call Nell. Something wasn't right and suddenly she questioned just how well she really knew Mack Dawson. Of course she knew him since the day her father brought her into town. Seen him on hundreds of occasions, but suddenly she realized they had barely exchanged more than fifty words in twenty years. The man she had seldom seen drink was jailed for public intoxication. He seen Jake and Felicity, and Sam knew in her heart, Jake was no killer.

"So you know what shifts I work," Mack's eyes glazed over unnaturally. She started to slow down, flipped the blinker.

"Took a few days off," he quickly replied. "I'm entitled aren't I?" The hairs on the back of her neck bristled as if tone became more taunt. If the car in front of her wasn't Sunday driving, she could be in David's driveway already.

"Tell me Sam, did you ever forgive Dale, you know for making you look bad?"

"Mack, that's kind of personal. But yes, I have."

"Why would you forgive a man for doing that to you? He deserved what he got, don't ya think?" Before she could unload how out of line he was speaking, she saw it. The shiny black metal with capability of taking life was pointing directly at her.

"Mack," her voice pitched. Reality slammed into her harder than a bolt of lightning. Her vision blurred with tears as she searched for a place to pull over.

"Keep driving," he ordered. "You owe me for that one." What was he saying?

"You? It was an accident," Sam shuttered.

"There are no accidents in this world. Turn here," Mack ordered next waving the gun left. When the gun went into her side, a brute act enforcing compliance, Sam jerked, causing the truck to swerve. Mack reached over and corrected the wheel. "No crashing or this will all be over too soon." He said shoving the hard metal into her side firmer.

"You?" Nausea waved over her.

"Me," he confessed with an arrogant smile.

Panic rising, Sam could only hope Cindy would get word to Quinn that Mack was with her. driving her home. She had no idea what Mack had planned, didn't want to imagine it considering what she did know. Short, overwhelming breaths overtook her and she tried to rein them in. She swallowed the dry cotton in her mouth and thought of Quinn. How none of this would be happening if she had just waited. Now she was on her own, with a killer, and had no one but herself to rely on. Only thing Sam was sure of, she wouldn't go down with a fight.

"You could never have done what they are saying," she said between trembling lips, buying time. She slowed through the sharp curve. Hopefully someone would see them.

"I have done it for decades," he flaunted. "Doesn't take much to be smarter than them, or your warden, either. Turn left at the end." She took her time and thankfully he said nothing of it. The sharp pain in her side eased as he pulled back the pistol a few inches.

"Jake was already three sheets to the wind when I got there last night. He was always a dimwit but I was surprised he thought to lure Felicity home. He did me a favor acting stupid on that matter. Didn't take much to convince her I was the safer choice." Now, Sam didn't suspect it had. "I did that for you too. She wasn't my type."

"For me," she shot out, forgetting for the moment who held the gun. "Are you saying you killed my husband and Felicity?" Fresh tears began pouring from her eyes as fear enveloped every inch of her. Mack pulled a hankie from his pocket and brushed her cheek clear. When she jerked her face away, he gripped her chin with a warning.

"Stop acting a fool Samantha. You did this to yourself. You are the one who spotted me first," his deep tone sent ripples of nausea through her. Sam hadn't a clue what he meant by that statement, only that in his eyes and now hers, people were dead. Lives were lost because of something she did.

"You may not understand everything right now my love, but soon, you will."

CHAPTER TWENTY-FIVE

"It might not be connected. Our guy takes them and keeps them a while. This was quick." Dorsey said as Ron sent Quinn a quick text. It was best to keep him in the know. After all they would all soon be family, and having Quinn watch over Nelly and Brody and Sam right now felt better than one agent now that the other was standing beside him.

The truck came speeding down the road and screeched to a halt sending a wet mixture of mud and slush over his patrol car. Ron would normally say something to that, but he didn't blame Quinn's rush one bit.

"That was quick. I sent that text three seconds ago. You should be ticketed for that young man."

"What text," Quinn asked but quickly shook off the care. "Is it really Felicity?" Quinn asked.

"Yeah. She's been strangled and her body dumped over there," Ron pointed. They've gathered what they could. A few prints since the ground's still soft." Quinn watched as the local beauty queen's remains were being loaded into the EMS vehicle.

"I need to call Sam, her shift was over an hour ago." He tried calling again but service out this way was sketchy or not at all. "She sent a text saying she was safe and on her way home now." Quinn told that agent to deliver his message, not take his fiancee for a joy ride.

"Just found out," Dorsey closed in on them. He pocketed his phone and made a quick search through a handful of files. "Those background checks came back and the power plant had one less worker today." He pulled one from the center of the stack and waved it in front of both of them.

"How well do you two know Mack Dawson." Quinn stumbled over the question.

"Rolled in here at eighteen, worked at the flower shop until Bob Cane and Larry Foster got him a job at the plant." Ron added. Quinn's stomach began to tighten. He hadn't thought of Mack. The man was a shadow, always around but never drawing attention to himself. He knew Larry, Jake's missing father, and yet one never considered him a possible suspect. He was the man no woman felt threatened around. The do-gooder who rarely spoke and always lent a hand when it was needed.

"I know a little further back," Dorsey opened a vanilla file and began reading. "Looks like he was arrested twice for attempted kidnapping in Arizona when he was seventeen. Both his parents disappeared in the eighties, and he hopped around a few small towns until taking up permanent residence here."

"He works a DuPont shift," Quinn put in, "and is a bit of a loner."

Companies records show he takes two vacations a year." Quinn closed his eyes and waited. "The second weekend in May and a week each year at Thanksgiving."

"Puts him free during the abductions," Ron said. The Prater girl we questioned said the man who tried to take her a few years back drove a red pickup. He had a beard, short trimmed, blue green eyes, and blonde sandy hair. She said he kept asking her if her birthday was really the 22nd. She admitted to posting it on social media but having a stranger walk up to her is why she ran and reported it. Three days later twenty-year-old Abbie Schrock disappeared."

"He was at the Brick last night according to Jake," Ron informed, meaning he had already questioned him immediately.

Quinn ran his figures through his hair angrily. There were three agents at the house, but still no sign of Sam. He hated knowing she would be driving right through here, but getting her home was priority.

"Sam should be here any minute. One of your agents is bringing her back."

"I don't like the smell of this, boys." David said walking their way. The camera around his neck revealed he was helping collect evidence. Quinn looked when he thought he heard a vehicle approach.

Where was she? "We need to find Mack and fast," Quinn said with urgency. "Agent, could you check in with one of your men and find out if he got lost between here and the county courthouse."

"Mack?" David said. "We picked Mack Dawson up about two this morning for drunk and disorderly. I tossed him in a cell to sleep it off."

"What?" Quinn yelled. "You put him in the same room with Sam?" He tossed David a glare, putting his cell to his ear. "She's not picking up," Quinn said in a panic.

"Are you telling me it's Mack?" David asked and then folded over. Quinn thought he was going to get sick. "I thought..."

"Yeah Cindy dear, has Sam already left ?" Quinn watched with hopeful anticipation. Maybe she stayed put, helped answer the parade of calls that had to have been burning up the control center since the fire this morning.

Ron closed his eyes and Quinn felt his heart sink into his gut. "She did. And how long ago was that?" Ron growled, yanking his hat from his head before continuing. "Cindy I need you to listen to me carefully and work fast. I'll have Connie come in and help but right now my darling, I need you to put out a BOLO, be on the lookout, for a 1994 Ford, blue and gray or a 2002 Chevy full-size red truck. Add descriptions of both Samantha Quinn and Mack Dawson. This is a kidnapping, hostage situation, and our suspect is armed and dangerous." The more Ron spoke the further Quinn's knees weakened. Dorsey followed suit, barking orders to his men. Bodies scrambled, words blurred into the background, and fear he had never known crumbled him. He had failed. He made a promise, and he had let a monster take her.

"Eight-county-wide perimeter, cover the river too. Water patrol and Rangers, and get me a chopper from over in Mason to assist. He's not getting far." Dorsey barked into his phone.

"Come on buddy," Dave shook Quinn's shoulders. "We've got to keep it together. Let's go find the girl." Quinn nodded. He made a trade, his worry for anger. If Mack so much as touched on hair on her head, there'd be nothing left to arrest. Just because Quinn didn't like violence didn't mean he was incapable of handing out his own.

The moment they reached Brier Ridge, Mack had ordered her to pull over. He bound her wrist with a large zip tie similar to those Quinn kept on his person. Mack forced her to the passenger seat and then climbed behind the wheel proving he was now in control.

"No one will see us now, so I'll take over from here," he laughed. It had been a ruse getting her behind the wheel, because who would suspect her in danger, behind the wheel.

"Did you know this land once belonged to Mormons?"

A pendulum of emotions swirled in her as he went on about things of no consequence. She searched out the window as the forest grew thicker, more melancholy. All she needed was the right opportunity, and she would escape. Her future meant she couldn't simple ride along, wait to be killed. Sam had to fight and she had to survive.

"They burned witches just fifty feet from my cabin," he continued with pride swelling in his voice. Her eyes burned with tears. Hanging didn't sound any better than any other death and she blinked them back in rebellion. Sam had heard of the Rolph family and the social unrest of the late 1800's many times in school and whenever Halloween came around. Slowly she inched her fingers to the door handle. She eased her body in slow meticulous moments to block her intentions as Mack continued talking about the woman who killed a whole passel of hogs by simply cursing them.

When the truck started up a steep grade, she took her shot at freedom. She knew these mountains, and if she could just get out, he would never catch her. With a yank of the handle, Sam leaped out. She rolled roughly but quickly got to her feet. She started to run as fast as her legs would carry her, tasting freedom just beyond the darkening forest.

"Now, now Samantha," he called out. She didn't dare turn and dodged between trees and brittle foliage. A pop sounded behind her, not slowing her pace. She could run to the old Folmer place. The judge was gone for winter, but he'd leave the cars. Suddenly a hand clamped onto her shoulders and the abrupt tackle had her on the ground.

He yanked her backward. the forty something man who didn't look to be capable of running a footrace had caught her. Her face planted in icy dirt and debris. Mack's body moved over her, his breath winded.

"Didn't think an old man capable, did ya?" he heaved and sucked in air as Sam wiggled and screamed below him. Using the only thing she could currently, she brought her knee up hard, striking him hard in the side. He let out a grunt before smacking her open handed.

"You can claw and bite and kick all you want. I don't feel pain, but if you try running again, you will," he threatened seconds before the needle punctured her flesh. Yanking her back to her feet and tossing her over one shoulder Sam felt her muscles deceive her.

She felt so heavy, lifting her arms to claw him next to impossible. She felt herself drift, but she wouldn't go to sleep. Whatever he injected in her was preventing her ability to fight, but not from hearing or seeing that he was packing her back to his truck.

"Get some rest darling, we have a lot of catching up to do," he said as she felt herself drift along the current of whatever fate awaited her.

He hadn't put her to sleep, but now Sam wished he had. When they pulled up to the old cabin, a new wave of fear worked through her, but she still wasn't herself.

"Diazepam," he said before getting out. With a jerk, her door came open. "Should wear off soon. I didn't even give you as much." He laughed, mocking her low tolerance to wicked things.

"I knew you would run, they usually don't, but I knew you would." Grabbing both knees, he turned her towards him and dragged her of the seat. Sam tried resisting, fighting against his brute force but found herself outmatched. Weak, she felt so weak.

"Now let's see if you've got your legs back," he said as if nurturing despite his death grip on her arms. She stood soundly and the fuzziness in her head was slowly leveling too. She could try to escape again, but taking that first step, she knew her legs wouldn't carry her far just yet. Still, for Brody's sake, she had to try.

"No one knows about this place. Might as well wrap your head around it darling, you're here now." When she made a lunge sideways, Mack slammed her against the truck. Watery blue eyes narrowed on her as he tightened his grip.

"Don't be stupid. I don't want to have to shoot you, not after waiting all this time. Don't test me Samantha, I'll do what I have to," he challenged. She believed him. A man capable of doing what he had already done didn't make threats lightly.

Yanking her towards the cabin, he didn't slow until they were inside. The only light sweeping across the house was reflected off the trace of snow covering the ground outside. They crossed a small sitting room full of covered furniture and dust that spoke of forgotten attention. She couldn't stop the tears and they seemed to make Mack's eagerness grow the more that fell. Not willing to give him extra ammunition, she willed them back. Anything to buy her more time. There was a good chance no one would find her in time, just as he said. If she was on her own, Sam needed to take every opportunity, every defense she could find, to escape. The silent prayer was for strength. She needed to trust He would give her enough strength to get away. Even if Quinn now learned of her disappearance, would he even know about the cabin?

When they reached the kitchen, he shoved her into the counter and rummaged through her coat pockets. "Where is it?" he growled anxiously. He slid his hand across her backside causing her to fight, but two hands quickly spun her around and subdued her, her face planted roughly against the filthy counter top. Dust swirled up and into her nostrils, collecting on the moisture her previous fears invoked. At least she felt her muscles gaining some ground. That was good, she collected.

Mack pulled the cell phone from her back pocket and then spun her back around before dropping it to the floor and smashing it under his dark tennis shoes. That lifeline was just another point in his favor. She searched wildly about for anything she could use against him, but only a tea cup, cracked and fragile was within her reach.

"Can't have the distraction in case your fiance decides to call. We got a lot of ground to cover you and I," he smiled greedily and yanked open a narrow yellow door beside her. "I had wanted to introduce you to them, but I guess that meeting isn't happening now."

A thin tunnel glowing a faint red sunk into the earth. "Go on down," he ordered. Her stance revealed she intended to fight if she had to. He thought it cute.

"Mack you don't have to do this. You could just leave me here and run. You might get away," she begged. He only laughed at her attempts and pushed her harder but Sam turned, bracing herself in the doorway.

"Thought you would be begging," he nudged her again, but Sam held her ground. "Step down, they are steep. Can't have you falling and killing yourself now can I." He laughed again.

The smell was horrid, like cold compost and rotted table scraps. Whatever loomed below she couldn't fathom and fear wrapped a cold hand around her heart.

She thought of Brody, of Quinn, and of the children just hours ago she had been dreaming of. Her personal fears shifted for those who needed her most. She would find a way. She would survive or die fighting.

At the sound of a sparking click a closer red light eerily lit her path. She still didn't budge. Mack wrapped a hand around her hair and pulled it into a tight hold. The gun he had pocketed now shoved in her back.

"Go Samantha, or I'll make you." When she refused, Mack shoved her harder this time and she nearly fell if not for one leg landing solid on the lower step. Taking advantage of catching her off balance, Mack continued bullying her forward.

At the bottom of the wooden stairs he shoved her forward, releasing his hold. She stumbled to collect herself, planting both palms against a wall for support. When her eyes lifted, there they were, all of them and more. From ceiling to knee, pictures of faces that had been splattered over newspapers and social media for three weeks. She gasped in horror, her heart tearing as the racing beat ran out of control.

"Don't you like my pictures Samantha? This was Chrystal Beckett. She turned thirty-two just two days before I met her. She has your eyes." Her breath ceased as his fingers traced the lining of her face and the ghostly blue pearls looking back at her. "Now Debbie here, she was a gift. I didn't have to go surfing the web for that jewel. The sweetest waitress in all of West Virginia. She had a bit of spunk like you do. Sweet Ivy," he growled running his fingers down a picture of a child, barely a teen. "She had your hair. You don't wear your hair like that anymore Samantha." His disapproving glare sliced into her.

"Why them?" she asked while panting breathlessly , but he ignored her to continue his game of cat and mouse.

"You have no idea how many times I wanted to tell you to stop cutting it, butchering those sweet locks," he ran his fingers through her hair, breathed it in. Acidy bile rose in her throat and she willed it back.

"Then why didn't you do it sooner!" She screamed at him. He had taken Nelly's child, her friend.

"It was you I wanted, but you and Jake were arguing in the doorway." When her eyes went wide he chuckled. "Yes, I think she is starting to figure this all out," he spoke to no one.

"Becky thought he kissed another girl and was upset that night. That's why she was outside crying." She remembered it now, cuddling her best friend, angry at Jake. So angry she stormed back inside the roller rink and fought with Jake in the doorway. He was just rounding the corner outside, searching Becky out to deliver an apology, when they heard the scream, that hard slam of a door. Everything after that happened so fast, but Sam still remembered each detail.

"That dumb kid was always getting in my way." Mack moved to a far corner and she noted he was searching for something. She glanced at the only way out. If only the room were smaller she'd run now, but his aim even if poor, wouldn't miss.

"Always hoped Larry would just knock him off and be done with it, but that was his mistake."

"You killed Jake's father too," she lifted her chin a little higher.

"That was easy. Two bottles of the good stuff and I took my time." A self satisfactory smile smeared over his face.

"No matter, I have you now don't I Samantha." He revealed a set of handcuffs and she backed herself to the wall and searched wildly for something to use against him.

"All of you. Every detail that has tempted my senses since I was twenty-two."

"I won't go easy Mack. Count on that," she insured and reached out for the tiny garden tool shovel laying on an old freezer.

"I hadn't planned on easy. That's what those are for," he motioned to freezer but she knew what lived in there and didn't take her eyes off him.

The sound of vehicles reached the cabin and Mack flinched. Sam didn't hesitate and used the opportunity to rush him. She could hear the front door burst open and thunder of footfalls above as Mack struck her hard. Ignoring the pain she clawed and stabbed at him but he twisted the tool from her clutch before slamming her into the wall. Sam felt the air knocked out of her, but willed herself to continue fighting. When she looked up from the ground, his gun was aiming right at her.

"Well darling, if I can't have you, neither will he."

Mack clicked off the safety just as the sound of rushing cattle came barreling down the stairs. At the sight of Quinn, Sam feared something much worse than death. Mack pivoted to change his aim.

"No Quinn," Sam cried out but Quinn didn't slow in her warning. Like the walls she had put up around her heart all these years, he marched right through without a hesitation.

The shot rang loudly, a forever echo ringing through the air. There was no way Mack missed this close, but before she could scoop up the garden tool and move on Mack herself, Quinn had Mack on the ground, pounding those heavy fists repeatedly into the monster below him.

Quinn had him, and she backed up when more men appeared at the top of the landing. One hit turned to ten and Quinn wasn't stopping just as David reached him, his gun drawn.

"Quinn stop!" He didn't. Holstering his gun David tried pulling him off the lifeless body, but even with all those extra pounds and few inches, David barely made a dent.

Sam watched in strange horror as the gentle man who played cars in the hallways and taught boy scouts in summer, unleashed a fury she had never knew in him.

Sam reached his side and called out, "Henry Owen!"

Quinn froze mid-punch and turn to her. "I'm okay baby," Sam said with frightened tears. His chest heaved and those dark eyes did hold danger, but slowly Sam could see recognition come back . Quinn looked down at what he had done and let out a rugged breath. Mack Dawson didn't move, nor pose a threat any longer.

"Come on brother, he's done." David touched his shoulder but he still didn't budge. Sam moved to him and bent forward. Cupping both hands on his face, she forced him to see her.

"Come on Henry," she urged. "I want to go home now." With that, Quinn let a long breath and slowly staggered to his feet. "Let me get that," he pulled a knife from his belt and though his bloody hands shook, he cut the tie binding her wrists together. More men descended the stairs but Sam didn't take her eyes off of him, nor he off her.

People say they would take a bullet for you, but few really would if put in a situation to choose. Henry was one of the few. He could have died, and yet, he just kept coming. There was no safer place on the planet for the rest of what days God seemed merciful to grant her, than in this man's arms.

"You found me," she whimpered and wrapped her arms around him.

"Took a little longer than I thought, sorry," he said pulling her close to his chest. Sam held on just as tightly as the little cellar room began crowding. Only now did she hear the sirens. When they faced each other again, Quinn winced and touched her cheek. She knew she sported bruises and a bloody lip, but that didn't compare to the alternative. She gave him a quick study too and noted the blood on his sleeve.

" You're hurt," he winced.

"And you have been shot," she replied. "Let's get you to a doctor before you have to break that promise, Warden. Can't have you getting married with a hole in your arm now can I?"

The End

Mindy Steele

ABOUT THE AUTHOR

Raised in Kentucky timber country, Steele is a best-selling and award winning author who writes in favor of her rural surroundings. Her books are peppered with humor, and sprinkled with grace, charming all the senses to make you laugh, cry, hold your breath, and root for the happy ever after ending. A storyteller at heart, she enjoys coffee indulgences, week end road trips, and researching her next book. Mindy is yepresented by Julie Gwinn of the Seymour Agency.

Website
www.mindysteeleauthor.wordpress.com

Facebook
www.facebook.com/mindy.h.steele

Instagram
www.instagram.com/msteelem07

Goodreads
www.goodreads.com/author/show/14181261.Mindy_Steele

Amazon
www.amazon.com/author/mindysteele

Twitter
www.twitter.com/mindysteele7